THE WORLD OF ASTRID LINDGREN

Pippi

LONGSTOCKING

in the South Seas

OXFORD
UNIVERSITY PRESS

Great Clarendon Street, Oxford OX2 6DP
Oxford University Press is a department of the University of Oxford.
It furthers the University's objective of excellence in research, scholarship,
and education by publishing worldwide. Oxford is a registered trade mark of
Oxford University Press in the UK and in certain other countries

© Text: Astrid Lindgren 1948/ The Astrid Lindgren Company 2020

First published in 1948 by Rabén & Sjögren, Sweden as *Pippi Långstrump i Söderhavet*.
For more information about Astrid Lindgren, see www.astridlindgren.com
All foreign rights are handled by The Astrid Lindgren Company, Lidingö, Sweden.
For more information, please contact info@astridlindgren.se

Pictures by Mini Grey
Translated by Susan Beard

ISBN: 978-0-19-277633-4

1 3 5 7 9 10 8 6 4 2

Printed in India

Pippi
LONGSTOCKING
in the South Seas

BY ASTRID LINDGREN
ILLUSTRATED BY MINI GREY
TRANSLATED BY SUSAN BEARD

OXFORD
UNIVERSITY PRESS

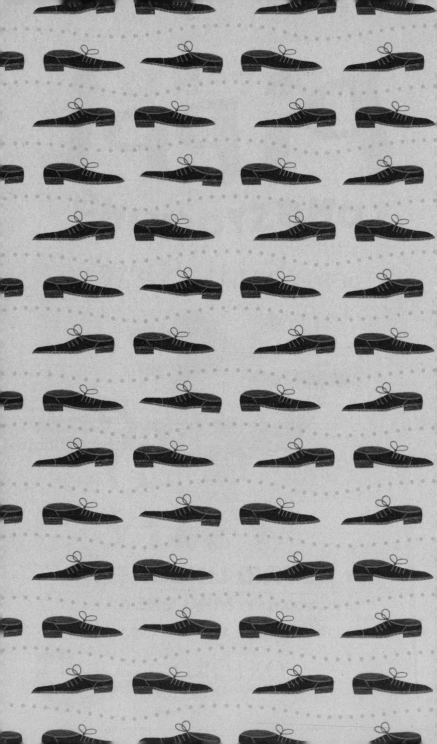

CONTENTS

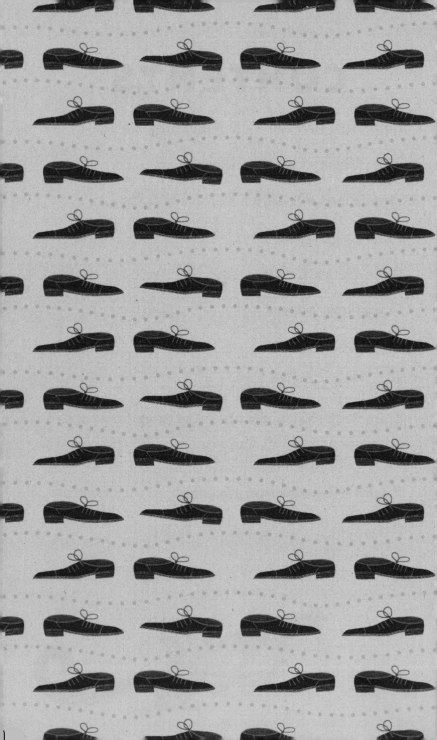

PIPPI STILL LIVES IN VILLA VILLEKULLA

The tiny little town looked very neat and friendly with its cobbled streets and its low houses surrounded by their flower beds. Everyone who went there was sure to think it must be a very calm and restful place to live. But there weren't many interesting sights worth seeing in the town. Apart from two: a local museum and an old burial mound. That was all. Well, there was one more thing. The people of the little town had very helpfully put up signs for anyone who wanted to see these special things. *To the Local History Museum* it said in large letters on one sign, with an arrow underneath. *To the Burial Mound* it said on another sign.

There was one more sign. And it said:

TO VILLA VILLEKULLA

That sign had only just been put up. You see, quite a lot of people who had come to visit recently had asked the way to Villa Villekulla— much more often, in fact, than the way to the local history museum or the burial mound.

One beautiful summer's day a man came driving into town. He lived in a far bigger town and that is why he had the idea that he was better and more important than the people in the tiny little town.

And as if that wasn't enough, he also owned a very smart car and looked like a thoroughly splendid gentleman with his shiny shoes and a thick gold ring on his finger. So perhaps it wasn't surprising that he believed he was somebody terribly posh and distinguished.

He sounded his horn loudly as he drove through the streets of the little town, so that people would notice him coming.

TO THE LOCAL HISTORY MUSEUM

TO THE BURIAL MOUND

TO VILLA VILLEKULLA

When that fine gent noticed the signs his mouth widened into a broad grin.

'*To the Local History Museum.* Must be my lucky day,' he said to himself. 'I'll be sure to give that a miss. *To the Burial Mound,*' he read on another sign. 'It gets better and better, I see.'

'But what kind of nonsense is that?' he said, when he saw the third sign. '*To Villa Villekulla . . .* what a name!'

He considered it for a while. A house could hardly be the kind of sight worth seeing like a local history museum or a grave mound. The sign must have been put there for a different reason, he thought. Finally he came up with a good explanation. Of course, the house was for sale. The sign had been put up for people who wanted to buy the house, to show them the way. The fine gent had been thinking for some time that he would like to find a house in some little town or other where there wasn't as much hustle and bustle as in the big town. He wouldn't live here all the time, naturally, but he would come and stay for a rest now and then. And in a small town it would be much more obvious that he was a particularly fine and distinguished person.

He decided to drive on and take a look at Villa Villekulla right away.

All he had to do was follow the direction of the arrow. He found himself driving all the way out to the edge of the little town before he found what he was looking for. And there—on a very dilapidated garden gate—someone had written, in red pen:

VILLEKULLA COTTAGE

Inside the gate was a wildly overgrown garden with old moss-covered trees, grass that needed cutting, and masses of flowers left to grow exactly as they pleased. Deep inside the garden stood a house, and oh my goodness, what a house it was! It looked as if it would collapse at any minute. The fine gent stared at the house and suddenly gave a gasp. *There was a horse on the veranda.* And the fine gent wasn't used to seeing horses on verandas. That was why he gasped.

Sitting on the veranda steps in the brilliant sunshine were three children. The one in the middle was a girl with a face covered in freckles and two red plaits sticking straight out. On one side of her sat a very pretty girl with fair curly hair and a blue-checked dress, and on the other a neatly combed boy. And on the red-haired girl's shoulder sat a monkey.

The fine gent thought for a while. He'd come the wrong way, hadn't he? Surely no one would think of selling such a dilapidated old house?

'Hey kids,' he called. 'Is this tumbledown old wreck really Villa Villekulla?'

The girl in the middle, the one with the red hair, stood up and started walking down the path. The other two trailed after her.

'Have you lost your tongue?' said the fine gent, before the red-haired girl had even reached the gate. 'Is this run-down place really Villa Villekulla?'

'Let me see,' said the red-haired girl, and she frowned deeply as she thought. 'Local History Museum—no! Burial Mound—no! I've got it!' she shouted. 'It's Villa Villekulla.'

'That's no way to answer,' said the fine gent, and got out of his car. He decided to have a closer look at the house anyway.

'We could always pull it down of course, and build a new place,' he muttered to himself.

'Oh, yes, let's start immediately!' shouted the red-haired girl, and quickly ripped a couple of planks from one wall.

The fine gent didn't listen to her. He wasn't the slightest bit interested in little children and at the moment he had something else on his mind. The garden in its overgrown state actually looked rather inviting in the sunshine. If you built a new house and cut the grass and swept the paths and planted proper flowers, even a very grand gentleman could live there. The fine gent made up his mind to buy Villa Villekulla.

He looked around to see if there were other things he could improve. Those mossy old trees would have to go, of course. He glared disapprovingly at a thick, knobbly old oak with its branches growing low over the roof of Villa Villekulla.

'I'll have that chopped down,' he said, firmly.

The pretty little girl in the blue-checked dress gave a cry.

'Oh, Pippi, did you hear that?' she said, sounding distressed.

The red-haired girl didn't seem to care and carried on practising her hop-skip-jumping up and down the garden path.

'Like I said, I'll be getting that dreadful old oak chopped down,' the fine gent said to himself.

The little girl in the blue-checked dress clasped her hands pleadingly.

'Oh, no, don't do that,' she said. 'It's . . . it's such a good climbing tree. It's hollow, and you can get inside it.'

'Don't be ridiculous,' said the fine gent. 'You

don't think I climb trees, surely?'

Now the neatly combed boy came up to him. He looked worried.

'But lemonade grows inside the tree,' he said, beseechingly. 'And chocolate too. On Thursdays.'

'Listen here, children, I think you've been sitting too long in the sunshine,' said the fine gent. 'It seems to have gone to your head. But that's got nothing to do with me. I'm thinking of buying this place. Can you tell me where I can find the owner?'

The little girl in the blue-checked dress started crying, and the neatly combed boy ran over to the red-haired girl, who was still practising her hop-skip-jumping.

'Pippi,' he said. 'Can't you hear what he's saying? Why aren't you doing anything?'

'Me, not doing anything?' replied the red-haired girl. 'Here I am, hop-skip-jumping till I'm blue in the face, and you come and tell me I'm not doing anything. Have a go yourself and tell me how easy it is!'

But she stopped jumping and walked over to the fine gent.

'My name is Pippi Longstocking,' she said.

'And this is Tommy and Annika.' She pointed at her friends. 'Is there anything we can do to help? A house to demolish or a tree to chop down or anything else that needs changing? Just say the word!'

'Your names are of no interest to me,' said the fine gent. 'The only thing I want to know is where I can get hold of the owner of this house. I intend to buy it.'

The red-haired girl, the girl called Pippi Longstocking, had started her hop-skip-jumping again.

'The owner is a little busy at the moment,' she said. She was concentrating tremendously hard on her jumping while she was speaking. 'Absolutely colossally busy,' she said, and jumped all round the fine gent. 'But sit down and wait a while and I'm sure she'll turn up.'

'She?' said the fine gent. 'Is a she in charge of this wretched house? So much the better. Womenfolk don't understand business matters. In that case let's hope I'll be able to get it all for peanuts.'

'We can always hope,' said Pippi Longstocking.

There didn't appear to be anywhere to sit

down, so the fine gent gingerly lowered himself onto the veranda steps. The little monkey scampered nervously backwards and forwards on the veranda railing. Tommy and Annika, the two sweet and neatly combed children, stood a short distance away and looked at him warily.

'Do you live here?' asked the fine gent.

'No,' said Tommy. 'We live in the house next door.'

'But we come here every day to play,' said Annika, shyly.

'We'll soon put an end to that,' said the fine gent. 'I don't want any kids running around my garden. There's nothing worse than children.'

'I agree,' said Pippi, and stopped jumping for a moment. 'All children should be shot.'

'How can you say that?' Tommy asked, indignantly.

'Yes, all children really should be shot,' said Pippi. 'But that wouldn't work. Because then there would be no one to grow up into dear little old chaps. And we can't be without them.'

The fine gent looked at Pippi's red hair and decided to try and be funny while he was waiting.

'Do you know the similarity between you and a

lighted match?' he asked.

'No,' said Pippi. 'But I've always wondered.'

The fine gent tugged one of Pippi's plaits hard.

'It's like this, you see. Both of them are burning on top, hahaha!'

'And I thought I'd heard it all,' said Pippi. 'How come I didn't think of that?'

The fine gent looked at her and then he said:

'Do you know something? I truly believe you are the ugliest kid I have ever seen.'

'Really?' said Pippi. 'You're not exactly a stunner yourself.'

The fine gent looked offended but he said nothing. Pippi was silent for a moment and looked at him with her head on one side.

'Mister,' she said. 'Do you know the likeness between you and me?'

'Between you and me?' said the fine gent. 'I certainly hope there isn't any likeness at all between us two.'

'There is,' said Pippi. 'We've both got ugly mugs. Except for me.'

A faint giggle came from Tommy and Annika's direction.

The fine gent's face turned completely red.

'Oh, you're impudent, are you?' he shouted. 'I'll soon beat that out of you!'

He aimed his thick arm in Pippi's direction but she instantly dodged aside and the next second there she was, up in the branches of the hollow oak tree. The fine gent could only gawp in amazement.

'When does the beating start?' asked Pippi, settling herself comfortably on a branch.

'I have time to wait,' said the fine gent.

'That's good,' said Pippi. 'Because I'm thinking of staying up here until the middle of November.'

Tommy and Annika laughed and clapped their hands. But they shouldn't have done that because by now the fine gent was boiling with rage, and since he couldn't get hold of Pippi he grabbed Annika by the scruff of her neck and said:

'Then I'll give you a good smacking instead. It looks like you could do with it too.'

Annika had never been smacked in her life and she gave a heartrending scream. There was a thud as Pippi jumped down from the tree. With one bound she was face to face with the fine gent.

'Oh no you don't,' she said. 'Before we start fighting I think I'd better teach you a lesson.'

And she did. She grabbed the fine gent around

his fat waist and threw him up in the air a few times. Then she carried him high above her head to his car and dumped him in the back seat.

'I think we'll wait for another day to knock this old shack down,' she said. 'You see, one day a week I knock houses down, but never on a Friday because then you've got the weekly cleaning to think about. That's why I always put the vacuum round on Fridays and knock it down on Saturdays. There's a time for everything.'

With great difficulty the fine gent crawled forward into the front seat and drove off at top speed. He was both afraid and angry, and it annoyed him that he hadn't been able to speak to the owner of Villa Villekulla. He really did want to buy the place and chase those nasty children away.

Quite soon he came across one of the little town's policemen. He stopped the car and said:

'Can you help me get hold of the lady who owns Villa Villekulla?'

'With the greatest of pleasure,' said the policeman. He leaped into the car and said:

'Drive to Villa Villekulla!'

'No, she's not there,' said the fine gent.

'Oh yes, I'm sure she is,' said the policeman.

The fine gent felt safe now that he had a policeman with him and he drove back to Villa Villekulla just as the policeman had suggested, because he was very keen to talk to the owner of the house.

'There's the lady who owns Villa Villekulla,' said the policeman, and pointed towards the house.

The fine gent looked where the policeman was pointing. Then he slapped his forehead and groaned. For there on the veranda steps stood the red-haired girl, that awful Pippi Longstocking, and she was holding her horse up in the air. The monkey was sitting on her shoulder.

'Come on, Tommy and Annika,' called Pippi. 'Let's have a quick ride before the next purstitcher turns up.'

'Purchaser, you mean,' said Annika.

'Is that . . . the owner of the house?' said the fine gent in a weary voice. 'But . . . she's only a little girl.'

'Yes,' said the policeman. 'She's only a little girl. The strongest girl in the world. She lives there all alone.'

The horse with the three children on its back came galloping up to the gate. Pippi looked down at the fine gent and said:

'You know, it was fun before, guessing those riddles. I know another one, by the way. Can you tell me the difference between my horse and my monkey?'

The fine gent wasn't in the mood for guessing any more riddles, but by now he had so much respect for Pippi that he didn't dare not to answer her.

'The difference between your horse and your monkey—no, I really don't know.'

'Well, it is a bit tricky,' said Pippi. 'But I'll give you a little clue. If you saw both of them together under a tree and one of them started climbing up the tree, then that one *isn't* the horse.'

The fine gent pressed the accelerator to the floor and drove off at full speed. He never, ever, returned to the little town again.

PIPPI CHEERS
UP AUNT LAURA

One afternoon Pippi was in her garden waiting for Tommy and Annika to look in. But no Tommy came, and no Annika either, and that is why Pippi decided to go and see where they were. She found them sitting among the lilac bushes in their own garden. But they weren't alone. Their mum, Mrs Settergren, was there too, along with a very sweet old lady who had come to visit. They were sitting there, just about to drink their coffee. The children had squash to drink.

Tommy and Annika hurried up to Pippi.

'Aunt Laura's here,' Tommy explained. 'That's why we didn't come to your house.'

'Oh, she looks so sweet,' said Pippi, peering through the lilac leaves. 'I really must go and talk to her. I like dear old ladies a lot.'

Annika looked a little worried.

'It's . . . it's probably not a good idea to talk too much,' she said. She remembered the time Pippi had come to a coffee party and had hogged the conversation so horrendously that Annika's mother had been really upset with her. And Annika didn't want anyone to be upset with Pippi because she was so fond of her.

'Not talk to her?' said Pippi, sounding offended. 'I jolly well will. People should be friendly when they go visiting. If I sit there sulking she might think I've got something against her.'

'But are you sure you know how to talk to old ladies?' Annika objected.

'You cheer them up, that's what you do,' Pippi said, confidently. 'And I'm going to do that right now.'

She walked up to the table among the lilac bushes. First she curtsied to Mrs Settergren, then she looked at the old lady and raised her eyebrows.

'Well, if it isn't Aunt Laura,' she said. 'And more beautiful than ever! Can I have some squash so my mouth doesn't go dry if we happen to start chatting?'

She said that last part to Tommy and Annika's mum. Mrs Settergren poured a glass of squash but as she did it she said:

'Children should be seen and not heard!'

'Hah! People have got both eyes and ears, I would hope. And even though I'm an absolute treat to look at, I definitely think ears benefit from a little exercise. But some people seem to think we've only been given ears to *wiggle*.'

Mrs Settergren didn't pay much attention to Pippi and turned instead to the old lady.

'And how is Aunt Laura these days?' she asked, in a sympathetic voice.

Aunt Laura looked worried.

'Oh, it's one thing after another,' she said. 'I'm so nervous and anxious about everything.'

'*Exactly* like my granny,' said Pippi, dunking a biscuit hard in her glass of squash. 'She got herself worked up and nervous over the tiniest thing too. If she was walking along the street and a roof tile happened to fall on her head, she'd jump about and make such a racket anyone would think there'd been an accident. And do you know, once she was with Dad at a ball and they were dancing the polka. Dad's pretty strong and all of a sudden he let go of Granny and she went flying right across the ballroom. She ended up sitting smack bang in the middle of the double bass. And hey presto, she started shrieking and making a racket again. Then Dad picked her up and held her out of the window, four floors up. Just to get her to calm down and not be so nervous. But do you think that worked? "Let go of me this instant," she yelled. So of course, my dad did. And guess what? She didn't like that either! Dad said he'd never known an old girl make such a fuss over nothing. Oh yes, it's not easy when people's nerves ache,' Pippi said sympathetically, dunking another biscuit.

Tommy and Annika squirmed in their seats. Aunt Laura shook her head, not knowing what to say, and Mrs Settergren said quickly:

'Let's hope you feel better soon, Aunt Laura.'

'Oh, I'm sure she will,' said Pippi, comfortingly. 'Because my gran did. She was as right as rain because she took something to calm her down.'

'What kind of something?' Aunt Laura asked, with interest.

'Fox poison,' said Pippi. 'One level tablespoon of fox poison. That did the trick, I can tell you.

20

After that experience she didn't budge an inch for five days and never spoke a word. Calm as a bowl of custard! Totally cured, in fact! No more squawking and leaping about. Roof tiles could come crashing down on her head one after the other, but she just sat there having a lovely time. So you see, Aunt Laura, you can get better, I'm sure. Because—as I mentioned—Granny did.'

Tommy had sidled up to Aunt Laura and whispered in her ear:

'Don't take any notice, Aunt Laura. She's only making it up! She hasn't got a granny.'

Aunt Laura nodded understandingly. But Pippi's hearing was good and she heard what Tommy had whispered.

'Tommy's absolutely right,' she said. 'I haven't got a granny. She simply doesn't exist. So why does she have to be so colossally nervous in that case?'

Aunt Laura turned to Mrs Settergren.

'Do you know, something very peculiar happened to me yesterday . . .'

'Well, it can't have been as peculiar as the thing that happened to me two days ago,' Pippi assured them. 'I was on a train and just as it was speeding along a cow came flying in through the open window, with a big suitcase hanging from its tail. She sat down on the seat opposite me and started flicking through the pages of the timetable to find out what time we would be arriving in Falköping. I was in the middle of eating a sandwich—I had tons with me, herring sandwiches and sausage sandwiches—and I thought she might be hungry, so I offered her one. And she took a herring sandwich and munched away.'

Pippi went quiet.

'That was certainly very peculiar,' said Aunt Laura, kindly.

'Yep, never known a cow like it,' said Pippi. 'I mean, fancy taking a herring sandwich when there were plenty of sausage ones!'

Mrs Settergren and Aunt Laura sipped their coffee. The children drank their squash.

'Well, as I was going to tell you before I was interrupted by our little friend here,' said Aunt Laura. 'There was the strangest coincidence yesterday . . .'

'Talking about strange coincidences,' said Pippi. 'I'm sure you'd like to hear about Agaton and Teodor. Once, when Dad's boat sailed into

Singapore, we needed another sailor on board. That's when we got Agaton. Agaton was two and a half metres tall and so thin his joints clattered like the tail of an angry rattlesnake when he walked. Raven-black hair he had, going all the way down to his waist, and only one gnasher in his mouth. But it made up for it in size because it went down to his chin. Dad thought Agaton was as ugly as a bag of spanners and he didn't want him on board at first, but then he said it would be good to have him in case they ever needed to set off a stampede of horses. Anyway, we got to Hong Kong and we needed another sailor, and that's when we got Teodor. Two and a half metres tall, he was, raven-black hair down to his waist, one single gnasher in his mouth. Actually, Agaton and Teodor were incredibly alike. Especially Teodor. In fact, they looked like twins.'

'That certainly was strange,' said Aunt Laura.

'Strange?' said Pippi. 'What was so strange about it?'

'That they were so alike,' said Aunt Laura. 'That really was strange!'

'No,' said Pippi. 'It wasn't a bit strange. Because they *were* twins. Ever since birth, in fact.'

She looked at Aunt Laura almost as if she was scolding her. 'I don't know what you're getting at, little Auntie Laura. Why argue and make a fuss just because two poor twins happen to look alike? They can't help it. And don't think for a single second, Aunt Laura, that anyone would look like Agaton of their own free will. Or Teodor either, for that matter.'

'Well, in that case,' said Aunt Laura. 'Why are you talking about strange coincidences?'

'If I could only get a tiny word in edgeways in the proceedings,' said Pippi. 'Then you would hear all about strange coincidences. Well, believe it or not, Agaton and Teodor walked about with their toes turned in, both of them. Ever so unnatural, it was. And with every step their right big toe bumped into their left one. And if that's not a strange coincidence I'd like to know what is! That's what the big toes thought, anyway.'

Pippi helped herself to another biscuit. Aunt Laura got up to leave.

'But Aunt Laura, you were going to tell us about that strange coincidence yesterday,' said Mrs Settergren.

'I think I'll save it for another time,' said Aunt

Laura. 'And now I come to think about it, it wasn't so awfully strange after all.'

She said goodbye to Tommy and Annika. Then she patted Pippi's red head.

'Goodbye, my dear,' she said. 'You're right. I think I'm starting to feel a little better. I don't feel nearly so anxious now.'

'Oh, I'm very happy to hear it,' said Pippi, and gave Aunt Laura a hearty hug. 'Do you know what, dear little Aunt Laura? My dad was really pleased when we found Teodor in Hong Kong because he said now he could scare twice as many horses.'

PIPPI FINDS
A SNIRKLE

One morning Tommy and Annika came skipping into Pippi's kitchen as usual and shouted good morning. Pippi was sitting in the middle of the kitchen table with Mr Nilsson, the little monkey, in her arms and a contented smile on her face.

'Morning,' said Tommy and Annika again.

'Can you believe it,' said Pippi, in a far-away voice. 'Can you believe *I'm* the one who made it up? Me and nobody else!'

'What have you made up?' asked Tommy and Annika. It didn't surprise them in the least that Pippi had made something up because she always did, but they wanted to know what it was. 'What exactly have you made up, Pippi?'

'A new word,' said Pippi, and she looked at Tommy and Annika as if she had only just seen them. 'A brand spanking new word.'

'What is the word?' asked Tommy.

'A most excellent word,' said Pippi. 'One of the best I've ever heard.'

'Tell us, then,' said Annika.

'Snirkle,' Pippi said triumphantly.

'Snirkle,' said Tommy. 'What does it mean?'

'If only I knew,' said Pippi. 'The only thing I do know is that it doesn't mean dustbin lid. Tommy and Annika thought for a while. At last Annika said:

'But if you don't know what it means then it's not much use, is it?'

'No, that's what annoys me,' said Pippi.

'Who actually thought up from the beginning what words mean?' Tommy wondered.

'Most likely a load of old professors,' said Pippi. 'And people are very odd, I must say. Think of the words they make up! "Tongs" and "plug" and "string" and stuff. No one has a clue where they get them from. But they haven't bothered inventing "snirkle", which is a really good word. How lucky I came up with it! And I expect I'll find out what it means, too.'

She contemplated this for a few moments.

'Snirkle! Could it possibly mean the very, very top of a blue-painted flagpole, do you think?' she said uncertainly.

'There aren't any flagpoles painted blue,' said Annika.

'No, you're right. In that case I haven't the faintest idea. Could it possibly be the sound you make when you trample in the mud and it comes up between your toes? Let's give it a try: "Annika trampled around in the mud and it made the most wonderful snirkle."' She shook her head. 'No, that doesn't work. "It made the most wonderful shblurp"—that's what it ought to be.'

She scratched her head.

'This is getting more and more mysterious. But I'll find out, whatever it is. Maybe you can buy it in a shop? Come on, let's go and ask.'

Tommy and Annika had nothing against doing that. Pippi went to find her travelling bag that was full of golden coins.

'Snirkle. Sounds expensive. I'd better take a whole golden coin.'

And so she did. Mr Nilsson hopped onto her shoulder as usual and then Pippi lifted her horse down from the veranda.

'No time to waste,' she said to Tommy and Annika. 'Let's ride. Otherwise there might not be many snirkles left when we get there. It wouldn't surprise me if the town mayor has already taken the last one.'

When the horse came galloping through the streets of the little town with Pippi and Tommy and Annika on its back its hooves clattered so loudly that all the children heard it, and they came out to run happily along beside it because they all liked Pippi very much.

'Pippi, where are you going?' they called.

'To buy a snirkle,' Pippi said, and pulled on the reins.

The children stopped running and looked baffled.

'Is it nice to eat?' a little boy asked.

'I should say so,' said Pippi, licking her lips. 'It's delicious. At least, it sounds like it is.'

She hopped off the horse outside a baker's shop and lifted down Tommy and Annika. In they went.

'I'd like a bag of snirkles, please,' said Pippi. 'The crunchy kind.'

'Snirkles,' said the pretty assistant behind the

counter, stopping to think. 'I don't think we've got any.'

'You must have,' said Pippi. 'Surely you can find them in every well-stocked shop?'

'Oh, well then, we've already sold out,' said the girl, who had never heard of snirkles but didn't want to admit that her shop wasn't as well-stocked as everyone else's.

'Does that mean you had them yesterday?' said Pippi excitedly. 'Please, please tell me what they looked like. I've never seen a snirkle in all my life. Did it have red stripes?'

The pretty assistant blushed charmingly and said:

'Oh dear, I don't know what they are! But we haven't got them here, anyway.'

Pippi walked back to the door, feeling very disappointed.

'Then I'll carry on searching,' she said. 'I'm not going home without a snirkle.'

The next shop was an ironmonger's. The assistant bowed to the children politely.

'I'd like to buy a snirkle,' Pippi said. 'But it must be the very best kind, the kind you kill lions with.'

The assistant looked crafty.

'Let me see,' he said, scratching behind his ear. 'Let me see.'

He found a garden rake and held it out to Pippi. 'Will this do?' he asked.

Pippi gave him a withering look.

'That is what educated people call a rake,' she said. 'But I happened to ask you about a snirkle. Don't try fooling a little innocent child!'

The assistant laughed and said:

'We haven't got one of those things you asked for, unfortunately. Try the haberdasher's on the corner.'

'The haberdasher's,' muttered Pippi. 'They won't have one there, I know *that* much.'

She looked gloomy for while, but then brightened up.

'Perhaps, when you think about it, a snirkle is an illness,' she said. 'Let's go and ask the doctor!'

Annika knew where the doctor lived because she had been taken there for her vaccinations.

Pippi rang the bell. A nurse came and opened the door.

'Is the doctor in?' asked Pippi. 'It's a very urgent case. A tremendously serious disease.'

'Do come in. This way,' said the nurse.

The doctor was sitting at his desk when the children came in. Pippi walked straight up to him, closed her eyes and stuck out her tongue.

'And what is the matter with you?' asked the doctor.

Pippi opened wide her clear blue eyes and pulled in her tongue.

'I'm afraid I've got an attack of the snirkles,' she said. 'I'm itching all over and my eyelids slam shut when I go to sleep. Sometimes I hiccup. And last Sunday I felt a bit poorly after I'd eaten a bowl of shoe polish and milk. Nothing wrong with my appetite but my food often goes the wrong way so it doesn't do me much good. I must have got an attack of the snirkles. Tell me one thing: is it catching?'

The doctor looked at Pippi's healthy little face and said:

'I think you are healthier than most. I'm certain you're not suffering from the snirkles.'

Pippi grabbed his arm, eagerly.

'So there is an illness called that?'

'No,' said the doctor. 'There isn't. But even if it did exist, I don't think it would give *you* any trouble.'

Pippi looked glum. She curtseyed deeply to the doctor by way of saying goodbye, and Annika did the same. Tommy bowed. Then they walked back to the horse that was waiting in the doctor's garden.

Not far from the doctor's house was a block of flats three floors high. A window on the top floor was open. Pippi pointed up at the open window and said:

'It wouldn't surprise me if there was a snirkle inside there. I'll pop up and have a look.'

And quick as a wink she shinned up the drainpipe. When she came level with the window she threw herself headlong into thin air and caught hold of the windowsill. She pulled herself up and thrust in her head.

Two ladies were sitting in the room inside, chatting. Guess how astonished they were to see a redhead suddenly appear above the window sill, and hear a voice saying:

'Just wondering, is there a snirkle in here?'

The two ladies shrieked in horror.

'Heavens above, child, what are you saying? Has someone escaped?'

'That's precisely what I would like to know,' said Pippi politely.

'Oh, perhaps he's under the bed?' cried one of the ladies. 'Does he bite?'

'Highly likely,' said Pippi. 'It sounds like he's got a good set of teeth.'

The two ladies clung to each other. Pippi scrutinized the room but finally said regretfully:

'No, not even a snirkle's whisker. Sorry for interrupting! I thought I'd enquire, seeing as I happened to be passing.'

She slid back down the drainpipe.

'Pity,' she said to Tommy and Annika. 'There's no snirkle in this town. Let's ride home again.'

And that's what they did. As they jumped down from the horse outside the veranda Tommy almost trampled on a little beetle that was scuttling along the gravel path.

'Oh, mind the beetle!' shouted Pippi.

All three crouched down to look at him. He was so small. His wings were green and gleamed like metal.

'What a beautiful little thing,' said Annika. 'I wonder what kind it is?'

'It's not a May beetle,' said Tommy.

'Or a dung beetle, either,' said Annika. 'And not a stag beetle. I really wish I knew what kind it was.'

A delighted smile spread across Pippi's face.

'I know,' she said. 'It's a snirkle.'

'Are you sure?' asked Tommy doubtfully.

'Do you think I can't recognize a snirkle when I see one?' said Pippi. 'Have you ever seen anything more snirkle-like in your life?'

Carefully she moved the beetle to a safer place where he wouldn't get trampled on.

'My sweet little snirkle,' she said, tenderly. 'I knew I'd find one in the end. But how odd. We've been running around town looking for a snirkle and there was one here all the time, right outside Villa Villekulla.'

PIPPI ORGANIZES
A QUIZ

The wonderful, long summer holidays came to an end one day and Tommy and Annika went back to school. Pippi still felt she was educated enough and didn't need to learn anything else, and insisted that she wasn't going to set foot in a classroom until the day she simply couldn't survive unless she knew how to spell the word 'seasickness'.

'Mind you, seeing as I never *have* seasickness, I hardly need to worry about the spelling,' she said. 'And if I ever happen to *get* seasickness I'll have more important things to think about than how to spell it.'

'You're never going to suffer from seasickness anyway,' said Tommy.

And he was right. Pippi had sailed the world's oceans with her dad before she ended up at Villa

Villekulla, but seasickness was something she had never suffered from.

Sometimes Pippi thought it was fun to collect Tommy and Annika from school on her horse. That always made Tommy and Annika very happy. They loved riding and there are certainly not many children who ride a horse home from school.

'Pippi, what about coming to meet us this afternoon?' Tommy said one day, just as he and Annika were on their way back to school after the lunch break.

'Yes, say you will,' said Annika. 'Because today's the day Miss Rosenblom will be giving out prizes to children who've been well-behaved and worked hard.'

Miss Rosenblom was a rich old lady who lived in the little town. She didn't like giving her money away but she did visit the school once a year to hand out gifts to the children. Not to all the children, oh no! Only the very well-behaved and hard-working ones. And to find out which children really were well-behaved and hard-working, she spent a long time asking them questions before handing out the gifts. That's why all the children in the little town lived in constant fear of her. Because every day, just when they were supposed to start their homework but were trying to think up something nicer to do, their mum or dad would say:

'Remember Miss Rosenblom!'

And it was hugely shameful to come home to parents and younger brothers and sisters the day Miss Rosenblom had visited the school and not have even the smallest coin or bag of sweets, or at least a vest. Yes, a vest! Because Miss Rosenblom also handed out clothes to the poorest children. But even being the poorest of the poor was no help if a child couldn't answer when Miss Rosenblom asked how many centimetres there are in a kilometre. No, it wasn't surprising that the children in the little town lived in constant fear of Miss Rosenblom. They were afraid of her soup, too! You see, Miss Rosenblom had all the children weighed and measured to see if any were especially thin and puny and looked as if they weren't getting enough food at home. Every one of those poor, thin little children could go to Miss Rosenblom's house every lunch break and eat a huge bowl of soup. That might have been wonderful for some of them, if only it wasn't for the nasty stuff floating about in the soup. It felt all slimy in their mouths.

But today was the great day when Miss Rosenblom would be visiting the school. Lessons finished earlier than usual and all the children gathered in the school playground. A big table was placed in the middle and at that table sat Miss Rosenblom. She had two secretaries who wrote down everything about the children: what they weighed, whether they answered the questions, whether they were poor and needed clothes, whether they had marks for good behaviour, whether they had little brothers or sisters at home who also needed clothes—there was no end to the things Miss Rosenblom wanted to know. On the table in front of her was a tin of money, masses of bags of sweets, and piles of vests, socks and woolly long johns.

'Everyone form lines!' shouted Miss Rosenblom. 'Line one, children without little brothers and sisters. Line two, children with one or two brothers and sisters. Line three, children with more than two brothers and sisters.'

Miss Rosenblom always wanted everything to be done properly, and it was only fair that children with lots of brothers and sisters were given bigger bags of sweets than those who had none.

Then the questioning began. Oh dear, how the children were shaking! The ones who couldn't answer had to first go and stand in a corner and feel ashamed of themselves, and then go home without so much as a single toffee to give their little brothers and sisters.

Now, Tommy and Annika were very clever at school. Even so, Annika was so nervous the bow in her hair was quivering as she stood in line next to Tommy, and Tommy's face grew whiter the closer he came to Miss Rosenblom. Just as it was their turn to answer there was a sudden commotion in the line for children without little brothers or sisters. Someone was pushing in front of all the children. And that someone was none other than Pippi. She shoved the children aside and walked right up to Miss Rosenblom.

'Excuse, me, I wasn't here at the beginning,' she said. 'What line do you stand in when you don't have fourteen brothers and sisters and thirteen of them are cheeky little boys?'

Miss Rosenblom looked very disapproving.

'You can stay where you are for now,' she said.

'But I imagine very soon you will be moving over to the line of children who will have to stand in the shameful corner.'

The secretaries wrote down Pippi's name and then she was weighed to see if she needed any soup. But she was two kilos too heavy.

'You will not be getting any soup,' said Miss Rosenblom sternly.

'What a stroke of luck,' said Pippi. 'Now all I've got to do is make sure I don't get any vests or long johns, then I can breathe a sigh of relief.'

Miss Rosenblom didn't hear her. She was searching in the dictionary for a difficult word for Pippi to spell.

'Listen to me, my girl,' she said. 'I want you to tell me how to spell "seasickness".'

'With the greatest of pleasure,' said Pippi. 'S-e-e-s-i-k-n-u-s.'

Miss Rosenblom gave a sarcastic smile.

'Really?' she said. 'The dictionary spells it quite differently.'

'Then how tremendously lucky that you wanted to know how I spell it,' said Pippi. 'S-e-e-s-i-k-n-u-s is how I always spell it, and it hasn't done me any harm.'

'Write that down,' said Miss Rosenblom to her secretaries, and pinched her lips together.

'Yes, do that,' said Pippi. 'Write down my perfectly good way of spelling it and make sure they change it in the dictionary right away.'

'Now, my girl,' said Miss Rosenblom. 'Answer this: when did King Karl XII of Sweden die?'

'Oh, no, has he died too?' cried Pippi. 'I must say, it's shocking how many people are popping off these days. I'm sure it wouldn't have happened if only he'd kept his feet dry.'

'Write that down,' said Miss Rosenblom, in an icy voice.

'Yes, why don't you?' said Pippi. 'And you can also write down that it's good to put leeches on your skin. And how you should drink a little hot paraffin oil at bedtime. It's a real pick-me-up!'

Miss Rosenblom shook her head.

'Why does the horse have stripes on its teeth?' she asked, solemnly.

'Hmm, are you sure he *has*?' said Pippi, thinking hard. 'You can ask him yourself, by the way. He's standing over there.' And she pointed to her horse that was tied to a tree.

She chuckled contentedly.

'What a good job I brought him here,' she said. 'Otherwise you would never have found out why he's got stripy teeth. Because, in all honesty, *I* haven't the faintest idea. And it's not something I bother about, either.'

By now Miss Rosenblom's mouth was a thin little line.

'This is outrageous,' she said. 'Utterly outrageous.'

'Yes, that's what I think too,' Pippi agreed. 'If I carry on being this clever I can't avoid getting a pair of pink woolly long johns.'

'Write that down,' Miss Rosenblom told her secretaries.

'No, don't bother yourselves,' said Pippi. 'I'm not exactly begging for some pink woolly long johns. That wasn't what I meant. But you can write down that I should be given a big bag of sweets.'

'I'll ask you one final question,' said Miss Rosenblom, and her voice sounded curiously strangled.

'Keep going,' said Pippi. 'I'm keen on quizzes like this.'

'Tell me this,' said Miss Rosenblom. 'Per and

Pontus are going to share a cake. If Per has a quarter, what does Pontus get?'

'A tummy ache,' said Pippi. She turned to the secretaries. 'Write that down,' she said, eagerly. 'Write down that Pontus got a tummy ache.'

But by now Miss Rosenblom had finished with Pippi.

'You are the most ignorant and rude child I have ever met,' she said. 'Go and stand in that other line this instant and be ashamed of yourself!'

Pippi trudged off obediently, but she muttered to herself:

'It's unfair! Why me? I could answer every single question too.'

After she had gone a few steps she suddenly remembered something, and she elbowed her way back to Miss Rosenblom.

'Excuse me,' she said. 'I forgot to give you my chest measurement and height above sea level. Make a note,' she said to the secretaries. 'Not that I want any soup—far from it—but we should at least keep the paperwork in order.'

'If you do not go at once and stand in that line and be ashamed of yourself,' said Miss Rosenblom, 'I know one little girl who will soon be getting a good spanking.'

'The poor kid,' said Pippi. 'Where is she? Send her to me, I'll protect her. Write that down!'

Then Pippi went and stood with the children who ought to be ashamed of themselves. Their mood wasn't especially lively. Many children were sniffing and crying at the thought of what their parents and brothers and sisters would say when they came home without money or sweets.

Pippi looked around at the crying children and gulped a few times. Then she said:

'Let's have a quiz of our very own!'

The children brightened up slightly but they didn't really understand what Pippi meant.

'Stand in two lines,' Pippi told them. 'Everyone who knows King Karl XII is dead in one line, and those who still haven't heard he's gone in the other.'

But because all the children knew King Karl XII was dead there was only one line.

'This won't do,' said Pippi. 'There have to be at least two lines or it's not right. Ask Miss Rosenblom, she'll tell you.'

She thought for a while.

'Now I've got it,' she said at last. 'Every fully

trained rascal stand in one line.'

'And who stands in the other line?' asked a little girl eagerly. She didn't want to be included with the rascals.

'The other line is for everyone who isn't a fully trained rascal *yet*,' Pippi said.

Over at Miss Rosenblom's table the questioning was still going on, and every so often a tearful little child wandered over to join Pippi's group.

'Here's a really difficult one,' said Pippi. 'Now

we'll see who has read their school books properly.'

She turned to a scrawny little boy in a blue shirt.

'You,' she said. 'Tell me someone who is dead.'

The boy looked a bit surprised at first, but then he said:

'Old Mrs Pettersson at number fifty-seven.'

'You don't say,' said Pippi. 'Do you know anyone else?'

No, the boy didn't. So Pippi cupped her hands

around her mouth and whispered loudly:

'King Karl XII of course!'

Then Pippi asked all the children in turn if they knew anyone who was dead, and they all answered:

'Old Mrs Pettersson at number fifty-seven and King Karl XII.'

'This quiz is exceeding all expectations,' said Pippi. 'Now I'll ask you one last question. If Per and Pontus are going to share a cake, and Per blankly refuses to have any at all and goes and sits in a corner to munch on a dry little crust, who will have to force himself to eat the whole cake?'

'Pontus!' shouted all the children.

'Have there ever been such clever children?' said Pippi. 'Now you get a reward too.'

And from her pockets she pulled out handfuls of golden coins and every child was given one. And every child was also given a large bag of sweets that Pippi took from her rucksack.

And that is why there was such joy among all the children who really ought to be ashamed of themselves. And when Miss Rosenblom's questioning was over and everyone could go home, no one ran faster than the children who had been standing in the shameful corner. But first they all crowded around Pippi.

'Thank you, thank you, Pippi. You're so kind,' they said. 'Thank you for the money and the sweets.'

'Don't mention it,' said Pippi. 'No need to thank me for those. But I did save you from pink woolly long johns, remember that!'

PIPPI GETS
A LETTER

The days went and autumn came. First the autumn and then the winter, a long cold winter that seemed as if it would never end. Tommy and Annika worked hard at school and for each day that passed they felt more and more tired and found it harder and harder to get out of bed in the mornings. Mrs Settergren grew quite concerned about their pale cheeks and poor appetite. To top it off they caught a case of the measles and had to stay in bed for a few weeks. It would have been a few very boring weeks if Pippi hadn't come over every day and performed tricks outside their window. The doctor had forbidden her to go indoors to see the children in case she picked up measles too, and Pippi obeyed, even though she said she could crush one or two billion measles

germs with her nails in one afternoon.

But no one said she couldn't do tricks outside the window. The children's room was on the first floor, so Pippi had propped a ladder up to the window. It was very exciting for Tommy and Annika to lie there in their beds and guess what Pippi was going to look like the next time she appeared on the ladder, because she looked different from one day to the next. Sometimes she was dressed up as a chimney sweep, sometimes she draped herself in a white sheet and pretended to be a ghost, and sometimes she pretended she was a witch. At other times she performed comical plays outside the window and played all the parts herself. Occasionally she did gymnastics on the ladder— and what gymnastics they were! She stood on one of the top rungs and swayed the ladder backwards and forwards, making Annika and Tommy scream in terror for fear she would go crashing down any second. But she didn't. When she climbed back to the ground she always went head first, just to make it look more amusing for Tommy and Annika. And every day she went into town and bought apples and oranges and sweets. She would put them all into a basket and tie a long piece of string to the handle. Then Mr Nilsson would climb up with the string and give it to Tommy, who opened the window and hoisted up the basket. Sometimes Mr Nilsson also came with a letter from Pippi, when she was busy and couldn't come herself. But that didn't happen often because Pippi entertained them on the ladder practically all day and every day. Sometimes she squashed her face up against the pane of glass and turned her eyelids inside out and pulled the most horrendous faces, and she told Tommy and Annika they could have a golden coin each if they didn't laugh at her. But that was completely impossible, of course. Tommy and Annika laughed so hard they almost fell out of their beds.

Eventually they got better and were allowed to get up. But my goodness, how pale and thin they were! Pippi sat with them in their kitchen the first day they were up and watched as they ate some porridge. Or rather, they should have been eating porridge, but it wasn't going at all well. Their mum grew very anxious as she saw them pushing the porridge around the bowl.

'Eat your lovely porridge, it'll do you good,' she said.

Annika stirred her spoon round and round the bowl but felt she couldn't swallow any more porridge.

'*Why* do I have to eat it?' she complained.

'*How* can you ask such a silly question?' said Pippi. 'Of course you have to eat your lovely porridge, so you can grow up big and strong. And if you don't grow up big and strong you won't be able to make *your* children, when you get any, eat *their* lovely porridge. No, Annika, this won't do. There would be nothing but porridge-eating chaos in this country if everyone thought the same as you.'

Tommy and Annika ate two spoonfuls each. Pippi watched them with great sympathy.

'You ought to spend some time at sea,' she said, rocking her chair backwards and forwards. 'You'd soon learn to eat. I remember a time when I was on my dad's boat and Fridolf, one of our crew, all of a sudden one morning ate only seven bowlfuls of porridge. Dad went insane with worry over his feeble appetite. "Fridolf, old matey," he said, choking back the tears, "I'm afraid you've picked up some kind of wasting disease. You'd better go and lie down in your bunk until you feel a bit livelier and can eat like normal folk. I'll come and tuck you in and give you some revitalising meducine!'"

'*Medicine*, you mean,' said Annika.

'So Fridolf staggered off to his bunk,' Pippi continued. 'He was worried himself and wondered what kind of awful bug he'd caught, seeing as he'd only managed to eat seven bowls of porridge. And as he was lying there, wondering if he would survive until evening, Dad came along with the meducine. Black and nasty, it was, but say what you like, it was revitalizing all right. When Fridolf swallowed the first spoonful it was like a tongue of flame shot out of his mouth. He gave a cry that shook the *Hoppetossa* from bow to stern and could be heard by ships fifty sea miles away. The cook hadn't had time to clear away the breakfast things when Fridolf came steaming in, yelling his head off. He threw himself down at the table and started eating porridge, and he screamed with hunger even after fifteen bowls of it. But by then the porridge was all gone, so the cook couldn't do anything except chuck a few cold potatoes into Fridolf's open mouth. As soon as he showed signs of stopping, Fridolf would start growling so fiercely the cook realized that if he didn't want to be eaten up himself he just had to carry on. But unfortunately he only had a measly 117 potatoes, and when he'd thrown the last one down Fridolf's throat he made a speedy leap out the door and locked it behind him. And we all stood outside, peering in at Fridolf through a window. He whimpered like a hungry baby and before we knew it he'd scoffed the breadboard and the jug and fifteen plates. Then he set about the table. He broke off all four legs and gobbled them down so the sawdust literally whirled around his face, but he said for asparagus it was a bit on the woody side. Seems he thought the table top was tastier because he smacked his lips as he ate it and said it was the best sandwich he'd had since he was a little lad. By this time Dad realized Fridolf had recovered from his wasting disease, so he went in to him and said if he could just hang on until lunch in two hours' time he would be given mashed swede and fried pork. "Aye aye, Captain," Fridolf said, wiping his mouth. "Just one more thing, Captain," he went on, his eyes shining eagerly. "What time is supper, and what about having it a mite earlier?"'

Pippi put her head on one side and looked at Tommy and Annika and their porridge bowls.

'Like I said, you ought to spend some time at sea. That would soon cure your feeble appetite.'

At that moment the postman walked past the Settergren's house on his way to Villa Villekulla. He caught sight of Pippi through the window and called out:

'Pippi Longstocking, I've got a letter for you!'

Pippi was so astonished she almost fell off the chair.

'A letter!? For me!? A lopper pretter—I mean, a proper letter!? I must see it before I believe it.'

But it *was* a proper letter, a letter with a lot of curious stamps on it.

'Read it, Tommy, you're good at that kind of thing,' said Pippi.

And Tommy read.

'My dear Pippilotta,' he read. 'When you get this you can go to the harbour any day now to look out for the *Hoppetossa*, because I'm on my way to bring you to the island of Koratuttutt for a while. You've got to have a look at the country where your father has been such a mighty king. It's really homely here and I'm sure you'll like it. And my faithful subjects are longing to see the famous Princess

Pippilotta. I won't hear another word—you are coming and that is my Kingly and fatherly desire. A whopping great kiss and much fondest love, from your old father,

King Ephraim I. Longstocking
Mighty Ruler of Koratuttutt Island.'

When Tommy had finished reading there was a deafening silence in the kitchen.

PIPPI GOES
ABOARD

And so one beautiful morning the *Hoppetossa* glided into the harbour, decorated with flags and pennants from bow to stern. The little town's brass band was assembled on the quayside, vigorously playing a welcome-home melody. Not one single person who lived in the town had stayed at home, and they were all gathered to see Pippi greet her father, King Ephraim I. Longstocking. A photographer stood waiting to take a snap of their first meeting.

Pippi was so impatient she was jumping up and down, and the gangplank had hardly been lowered before Captain Longstocking and Pippi threw themselves together with tremendous shouts of joy. Captain Longstocking was so glad to see his daughter that he threw her high above the ground a few times. And Pippi was just as heartily glad to see her dad that she threw him up in the air more than a few times. The only person who wasn't glad was the photographer, because it was impossible for him to take a proper picture when either Pippi or her dad were high up in the air.

Now it was Tommy and Annika's turn to go and welcome Captain Longstocking, but oh dear, how washed out and pitiful they looked! It was the first time they were out of doors after being ill, of course.

Naturally, Pippi had to go aboard and say hello to Fridolf and all her sailor friends. Tommy and Annika were allowed to go with her. It felt very special to stride about on a ship that had travelled from so far away, and Tommy and Annika looked around wide-eyed so as not to miss anything. They looked especially hard for Agaton and Teodor, but Pippi said they had been released from duty ages ago.

Pippi hugged all the sailors so hard it left them gasping for breath for a full five minutes afterwards. Then she lifted Captain Longstocking onto her shoulders and carried him through the crowds of people all the way home to Villa

Villekulla. Tommy and Annika trotted after her, hand in hand.

'Long live King Ephraim!' cried all the people, and they thought it was a great day in the history of the town.

A few hours later Captain Longstocking was fast asleep in his bed at Villa Villekulla, snoring so loudly that the whole house was shaking. Pippi, Tommy, and Annika sat round the kitchen table, with its remains of a bumper evening meal. Tommy and Annika were rather quiet and thoughtful. What were they thinking about? Well, Annika was thinking that perhaps, when it came down to it, you were better off dead. And Tommy was sitting there trying to remember if there was any fun left in the world, but he couldn't think of anything. The whole of life was more or less a desert, he thought.

But Pippi was in a splendid mood. She patted Mr Nilsson, who was stepping delicately among the plates on the table, she patted Tommy and Annika, she whistled and sang in turns, and every so often she twirled and skipped joyfully about. She didn't seem to notice that Tommy and Annika were downhearted.

'It'll be lovely to go to sea again for a time,' said Pippi. 'Think of being on the ocean, the freedom of it!'

Tommy and Annika sighed.

'And I'm actually rather excited about seeing Koratuttutt Island too. Imagine lying stretched out on the beach, dipping your big toes in the actual South Sea of all places, and all you have to do is open your mouth wide and a ripe banana drops into it.'

Tommy and Annika sighed.

'I think it will be such fun playing with those little Koratutt children,' Pippi went on.

Tommy and Annika sighed.

'What are you sighing for?' asked Pippi. 'Don't you like sweet little Koratutt children?'

'Ye-es,' said Tommy. 'But we can't help thinking it's likely to be a long time before you come back to Villa Villekulla.'

'Well, that's true,' said Pippi joyfully. 'But it doesn't make me at all sad. I think you can almost have more fun on Koratuttutt Island.'

Annika turned her pale, despairing face to Pippi.

'Oh, Pippi,' she said. 'How long will you be

away, do you think?'

'Hmm, that's not so easy to say. Until about Christmas, I expect.'

Annika wailed.

'Who knows?' said Pippi. 'It might be so much fun on Koratuttutt Island that I want to stay there forever. A Koratutt princess—that's not such a bad career for someone with as little schooling as I've had.'

Tommy and Annika's eyes began to look strangely shiny in their pale faces. And all of a sudden Annika leaned over the table and burst into tears.

'Still, when I come to think about it, I don't suppose I'll want to stay there forever,' said Pippi. 'You can have too much of the royal life and get a bit bored with all of it. So one fine day I expect I'll say: "Well, Tommy and Annika, what about moseying back home to Villa Villekulla for a while?"'

'Oh, it'll be super when you write and tell us that,' said Tommy.

'Write?' said Pippi. 'You've got ears in your head, haven't you? I won't be writing it, I'll be *saying* it, like this: "Tommy and Annika, now we're going home to Villa Villekulla."'

Annika raised her head from the table and Tommy said:

'What do you mean by that?'

'What do I mean? Don't you understand the Swedish language? Or could it be I've forgotten to tell you that you're coming with me to Koratuttutt Island? I was certain I'd mentioned it.'

Tommy and Annika shot up from the table and stood there, gasping. But then Tommy said:

'What are you talking about? Mum and Dad will never let us go.'

'Oh yes they will,' said Pippi. 'I've already spoken to your mum about it.'

There was silence in Villa Villekulla's kitchen for precisely five seconds. Then there were two deafening howls. It was Tommy and Annika, yelling their heads off in joy. Mr Nilsson, who was sitting on the table trying to spread butter on his hat, looked up in surprise. He was even more surprised when he saw Pippi and Tommy and Annika grab hold of each other's hands and start dancing wildly all over the room. They danced and shouted so much the ceiling lamp came loose and fell to the floor. But then Mr Nilsson threw the butter knife out of the window and joined in the dancing as well.

'Is it really, really true?' asked Tommy, after they had calmed down and climbed inside the log box to discuss the situation. Pippi nodded.

Yes, it was really true. Tommy and Annika were allowed to go to Koratuttutt Island with Pippi. Naturally, almost all the ladies in the little town came to have a word with Mrs Settergren, and said:

'*Surely* you're not thinking of sending your children far away to the South Seas with *Pippi Longstocking*? You can't mean it.'

But then Mrs Settergren said:

'Why wouldn't I? The children have been ill and need a change of air, so the doctor says. And for as long as I have known Pippi she has never done anything to cause Tommy and Annika any harm. No one could take more care of them than she does.'

'But *Pippi Longstocking*, of all people,' said the ladies, screwing up their noses.

'Exactly,' said Mrs Settergren. 'Pippi Longstocking may not always know the right way to behave, but she's got a good heart.'

♥

And so, one chilly evening in early spring, Tommy and Annika left the little, little town for the first time in their lives to travel at Pippi's side into the big, wondrous world. There they stood at the railing, all three, as the fresh evening breeze filled the sails of the *Hoppetossa*. All three—well, it would be more accurate to say all five, because the horse and Mr Nilsson were there too.

All the children's school friends stood on the quayside, almost crying with grief and envy. Tomorrow they would be going to school as usual. They were all studying the South Seas for their geography homework. Tommy and Annika weren't going to be doing any homework at all for quite some time. 'Their health has to come before their school work,' the doctor said. 'And they can learn about the South Seas by being there,' Pippi said.

Tommy and Annika's mum and dad were also there on the quayside, and the children felt a pang when they saw them dab their eyes with a hankie. But in spite of that Tommy and Annika couldn't help feeling so very, very happy that it almost hurt.

Slowly the *Hoppetossa* slid away from the quayside.

'Tommy and Annika!' shouted Mrs Settergren. 'When you get to the North Sea you must wear two vests and . . .'

The rest of what she wanted to say was drowned out by the cries of goodbye from the people in the harbour, the wild neighing of the horse, Pippi's joyful shouts and the powerful trumpeting from Captain Longstocking as he blew his nose.

The journey had begun. Out under the stars sailed the *Hoppetossa*. Floating pieces of ice danced around the bow and the wind sung in the sails.

'Oh, Pippi,' said Annika. 'I feel so funny inside. I'm starting to believe I'll be a pirate too, when I'm older.'

PIPPI GOES
ASHORE

'Koratuttutt Island ahoy!' shouted Pippi one sun-drenched morning, as she stood at the lookout wearing only a little piece of cloth for a skirt.

They had sailed for days and nights, for weeks and months, over storm-whipped seas and calm, friendly waters, by starlight and by moonlight, under dark threatening skies and in the burning sun—yes, they had been sailing for so long that Tommy and Annika had almost forgotten what it felt like to live in the tiny little town.

Their mother would surely have been astonished if she could see them now. No more pale cheeks! Healthy and suntanned and bright-eyed, they clambered about in the rigging just like Pippi. Their clothes had come off one layer at a time as the climate grew hotter, and the

two warmly-dressed children with two vests who had crossed the North Sea had turned into two small, brown, naked youngsters, each with a little cloth wrapped round their waist.

'Oh, how lovely this is,' said Tommy and Annika every morning, when they woke in the cabin they shared with Pippi. Often Pippi was already up and standing at the tiller.

'A better seafarer than my daughter has never sailed the seven seas,' Captain Longstocking always said. And he was right. Through the very worst shallows and over the most dangerous underwater rocks, Pippi steered the *Hoppetossa* with a steady hand.

But now the journey was almost at an end.

'Koratuttutt Island ahoy!' shouted Pippi.

Yes, there it was, under green palm trees and surrounded by the bluest waters.

Two hours later the *Hoppetossa* sailed into a narrow inlet on the island's west side. And there on the sand were all the Koratutts, men, women and children, ready to greet their king and his red-haired daughter. A loud roar rose up from the crowd of people as the gangplank was lowered.

'Ussumkura kussomkara!' they shouted, which meant:

'Welcome back, fat white chieftain!'

King Ephraim walked majestically down the gangplank, dressed in his blue corduroy suit, while on the foredeck Fridolf played the Koratutt national anthem on his accordion: 'Here come the hurly-burly Swedes!'

King Ephraim raised his hand in greeting and shouted:

'Muoni manana!' which meant:

'Nice to see you again!'

After him came Pippi. She was carrying the horse. A gasp went through the crowd of Koratutts. They had heard all about Pippi's colossal strength, of course, but it was quite a different thing to see it in real life. Tommy and Annika stepped dutifully ashore as well, and so did all the crew, but at that moment the Koratutts only had eyes for Pippi. Captain Longstocking picked her up and stood her on his shoulders so they could get a proper look at her, and another gasp rippled through the crowd. But the next minute Pippi picked up Captain Longstocking on one of her shoulders and the horse on the other, and then the gasp practically turned into a hurricane.

There were no more than 126 people living on Koratuttutt Island.

'That's just about the right number of subjects to have,' said Captain Longstocking. 'More than that and you can't keep track of them.'

They all lived in small, comfy huts among the palm trees. The largest and finest hut belonged to Captain Ephraim. The crew of the Hoppetossa had their own huts, where they lived while the Hoppetossa lay at anchor in the little bay. Which, by the way, she did for most of the time these days. Very occasionally it was necessary to make an expedition to an island 500 kilometres to the north, and that was because the island had a shop that sold the tobacco Captain Longstocking liked.

A very smart, newly-constructed hut under a coconut tree was meant especially for Pippi, and there was plenty of room for Tommy and Annika too. But before they could go into the hut and wash off the dust of the journey, Captain Longstocking wanted to show them something. He took hold of Pippi's arm and led her back to the beach.

'Here,' he said. 'It was here I floated ashore that

time I blew overboard into the ocean.'

The Koratutts had put up a memorial stone in honour of that remarkable event. On the stone was carved, in Koratuttish:

'From over the great, wide ocean came our fat, white king. This is the place where he floated ashore, when the breadfruit tree was blooming. May he always be as fat and splendid as when he came.'

Captain Longstocking read the inscription aloud for Pippi, Tommy, and Annika in a voice that trembled with emotion. Afterwards he blew his nose loudly.

When the sun began to sink and was about to disappear into the vast embrace of the South Seas, the drums of the Koratutts called everybody to the meeting place in the centre of the village where they had festivals and made decisions. There stood Captain Ephraim's impressive bamboo throne, decorated with red hibiscus flowers. It was where he sat when he governed the people. The Koratutts had already made a smaller throne for Pippi that stood next to her father's, and they had hastily put together two small bamboo chairs for Tommy and Annika.

The sound of the drums grew louder and louder

as King Ephraim took his place on the throne with great dignity. He had taken off his corduroy suit and was dressed in his royal garments, with a crown on his head, a grass skirt, a necklace of sharks' teeth and thick ankle bracelets. Pippi sat down comfortably on her throne. She was still wearing the same little cloth skirt but she had stuck a few red and white flowers in her hair to suit the occasion. Annika had done the same. But not Tommy. Nothing could persuade him to put flowers in his hair.

King Ephraim had been away from his ruling duties for rather a long time, so now he set about ruling as hard as he could. As he did so, the little Koratutt children crept closer to Pippi's throne. For some unimaginable reason they had the idea that white skin was finer than black, and that's why they felt more in awe of Pippi and Tommy and Annika the closer they came to them. And, of course, Pippi was a princess. When they had come as close to Pippi as they could, they all threw themselves onto their knees in front of her and bent their foreheads to the ground.

Pippi hopped swiftly down from her throne.

'What's this I see?' she said. 'Do you play at

being thing-finders too? Wait, I'll join you!'

She knelt down and searched around on the ground.

'Seems like there have been thing-searcherers here before us,' she said, presently. 'There's not so much as a safety pin here, I can assure you of that.'

She went back to her throne again. Hardly had she sat down before all the children once more bowed their heads to the ground in front of her.

'Have you dropped something?' Pippi asked. 'Well, it's not there, so you might as well get up.'

As luck would have it, Captain Longstocking had lived on the island for so long that some of the Koratutts had learned a few words of his language. Naturally, they didn't know difficult words like 'registered mail' and 'entrance fee', but they had managed to pick up quite a lot. Even the children knew the most common expressions, such as 'Don't touch that', for example. One little boy called Momo could speak their language really well, because he used to spend time down by the huts where the crew lived, listening to the men chatting. And a pretty little girl called Moana wasn't bad at it, either.

Momo tried to explain to Pippi why they were kneeling before her.

'You very fine white princess,' he said.

'I not at all very fine white princess,' said Pippi. 'I mainly only Pippi Longstocking and now I not give tuppence for this throning lark.'

She jumped down from her throne and so did King Ephraim, because he had finished the ruling business for now.

The sun sank like a red ball in the South Seas and soon the sky blazed with stars. The Koratutts built an enormous bonfire at the meeting place and King Ephraim, Pippi, Tommy, and Annika, and the crew of the *Hoppetossa* threw themselves down in the green grass and watched as the Koratutts danced round the fire. The dull beating of the drums, the strange dancing, the rare fragrance of a thousand unknown flowers deep in the jungle, the twinkling night sky overhead—all of it made Tommy and Annika feel quite funny inside. All the time the constant crash of the ocean waves could be heard as a mighty accompaniment.

'I think this is a very good island,' said Tommy afterwards, when they were tucked up in beds in their cosy little hut under the coconut tree.

'I think so too,' said Annika. 'Don't you, Pippi?'

But Pippi lay there silently, with her feet on the pillow the way she always did.

'Hear the roar of the ocean waves,' she said, dreamily.

PIPPI TEACHES
A SHARK A LESSON

Very early the next morning Pippi, Tommy, and Annika crawled out of their hut. But the Koratutt children had woken up even earlier. They were already sitting excitedly under the coconut tree, waiting for the white children to come out and play. They were chatting merrily in Koratuttish and laughing so much their teeth gleamed in their faces.

The whole group of children set off for the beach with Pippi leading the way. Tommy and Annika skipped in delight when they saw the beautiful white sand you could dig yourself down in, and the blue sea that looked so inviting. A coral reef not far out to sea acted as a breakwater for the waves, so that inside the reef the water lay as still and shiny as a mirror. All the children tore off their little strips of clothing and charged laughing and screaming into the water.

Afterwards, they rolled in the white sand and Pippi, Tommy, and Annika agreed that they would much rather have black skin because white sand looked so funny on a black background. But when Pippi dug herself down in the sand until only a freckly face and two red plaits stuck out, that looked pretty funny as well. The children sat down around her to talk.

'Tell us about white children in the white children's land,' Momo said to the freckly face.

'White children love multikipperation,' said Pippi.

'Multiplication, you mean,' said Annika. 'And you can't exactly say that we *love* it.'

'White children love multikipperation,' Pippi insisted. 'White children go bonkers if white children not get big dose multikipperation every day.'

Then she couldn't be bothered speaking jumbled-up Koratuttish any longer, so she switched to her own language.

'If you hear a white child crying you can be sure their school has burned down or a day- off has been announced, or their teacher has forgotten to give them any multikipperation homework. And don't talk about the summer holidays. There's such a crying and moaning you'd rather be dead than have to listen to it. And there's never a dry eye when the schools shut their doors for the summer. All the children drag themselves home, singing mournful songs and sobbing like they've got the hiccups, because they know it will be months before they'll be doing any multikipperation again. Honestly, you've never seen such misery,' Pippi said, sighing deeply.

'Uhh,' groaned Tommy and Annika.

Momo didn't quite understand what multikipperation was and he wanted an explanation. Tommy was just about to tell him when Pippi got in first.

'Well, you see,' she said, 'it's like this: 7 times 7 is 102. Clever, eh?'

'It certainly isn't 102,' said Annika.

'No, because it's 49,' said Tommy.

'Remember, we're on the island of Koratuttutt,' said Pippi. 'It's quite a different and more fruitful kind of climate, so 7 times 7 is much more here.'

'Uhh,' groaned Tommy and Annika.

The arithmetic lesson was interrupted by

Captain Longstocking, who came to tell them that he and his crew and all the Koratutt islanders were going to set off to another island to hunt wild pigs for a few days. Captain Longstocking was in the mood for a fresh pork chop. The Koratutt women were going along as well, so that they could scare the pigs into the open with their wild screaming. That meant the children would be left alone on Koratuttutt Island.

'You won't be sad, will you?' asked Captain Longstocking.

'Give you three guesses,' said Pippi. 'The day I hear that some children are sad because they've been left to look after themselves without any grown-ups is the day I learn every single multikipperation table backwards, I swear.'

'That's what I like to hear,' said Captain Longstocking.

And with that he and his subjects, armed with their shields and spears, piled into their long canoes and paddled away from Koratuttutt Island.

Pippi cupped her hands like a loudspeaker and shouted after them:

'Safe journey! But if you're not back in time for my fiftieth birthday I'll send out a search party.'

Now that they were alone, Pippi and Tommy and all the other children looked at each other contentedly. Here they were with a whole South Sea island all to themselves for a few days.

'What shall we do?' asked Tommy and Annika.

'First we'll get breakfast down from the trees,' said Pippi.

And she clambered nimbly up a palm tree to fetch coconuts. Momo and the other Koratutt children picked breadfruits and bananas. Pippi made a fire on the beach and she roasted the delicious breadfruit. The children sat in a ring around her and all of them ate a hearty breakfast consisting of roasted breadfruit, coconut milk and bananas.

There weren't any horses on Koratuttutt Island, which is why all the Koratutt children were extremely interested in Pippi's horse. Those who dared could have rides on him. Moana said she really wanted to visit the land of the white people where there were such strange animals.

There was no sign of Mr Nilsson. He had taken himself off on a little excursion into the jungle, where he had found a number of his relations.

'What shall we do now?' asked Tommy and

Annika, when it was no longer quite so much fun riding the horse.

'White children want see good caves, yes, no?' said Momo.

'White children definitely want see good caves, yes, yes,' said Pippi.

Koratuttutt Island was a coral island. On its southern side steep coral walls plunged straight down into the sea, where there were the most wonderful coral caves, carved out by the sea. Some of them were down on a level with the water, but there were some higher up the cliffs and that's where the Koratutt children used to play. They had hidden a huge store of coconuts and other tasty things in the largest cave. Getting there was a tricky business. You had to climb extra carefully across the steep cliff face, hanging on to protruding rocks and little ledges, otherwise it would be easy to fall into the sea. That wouldn't normally matter much, of course. But the only thing was, the water was full of sharks that loved to eat little children. In spite of this the Koratutt children used to have fun diving for oysters, but one of them had to stand guard and promise to shout, 'Shark, shark!'

the minute a shark fin was seen. Inside the big cave the Koratutt children had gathered a store of gleaming pearls that they had found inside the oysters. They used them to play marbles. They hadn't the faintest idea that these pearls were worth no end of money in the white man's countries. Captain Longstocking always took a few with him when he went to buy snuff. The pearls bought him loads of things he thought his subjects might need, but on the whole he thought his faithful Koratutts were quite happy the way they were. So the children were more than welcome to go on playing marbles with the pearls.

Annika refused outright when Tommy told her to climb across the cliff wall to the big cave. The first part wasn't too bad because there was quite a wide ledge to walk on, but it gradually became narrower and narrower, and for the last few metres before the cave you had to cling on and use whatever footholds you could find.

'Never,' said Annika. 'Not me!'

Scrambling across a cliff face with hardly anything to hang on to and ten metres below a sea full of sharks only waiting for someone to fall in—that wasn't what Annika called fun.

Tommy was angry with her.

'Huh, never bring your sister with you to a South Sea island,' he said, as he clung to the cliff face. 'Look at me! All you have to do is this . . .'

Plop. That was Tommy tumbling into the sea. Annika screamed loudly. Even the Koratutt children were terrified.

'Shark, shark!' they shouted, and pointed out to sea. A fin was sticking out of the water and

heading straight for Tommy.

Plop. This time it was Pippi, jumping in. She reached Tommy at almost exactly the same time as the shark. Tommy was so frightened he was yelling his head off. He felt the shark's teeth graze his leg. But at that moment Pippi grabbed the bloodthirsty brute with both hands and lifted him out of the water.

'Have you completely forgotten your manners?' she said. The shark looked around in astonishment, feeling rather uncomfortable. He couldn't breathe terribly well out of the water.

'Promise never to do that again and I'll let you go,' said Pippi sternly. And with all her strength she threw the shark far out to sea. He couldn't wait to get away from there and decided to swim as fast as he could to the Atlantic Ocean instead.

By this time Tommy had clawed his way onto a tiny ledge and was sitting there, quivering all over. His leg was bleeding. Then Pippi came over to him. She was acting very strangely. First she lifted Tommy up in the air and then she hugged him so hard that almost all the air was squeezed out of him. Then all of a sudden she put him down, sat on the ledge and hid her face in her hands. She was crying. Pippi was crying. Tommy and Annika and all the Koratutt children looked at her in amazement and dismay.

'You cry because Tommy might get eat up,' Momo suggested.

'No,' snapped Pippi, wiping her eyes. 'I cry because poor little hungry shark get no breakfast today.'

PIPPI TALKS
SENSE INTO
JIM AND BUCK

The shark's teeth had only grazed the skin on Tommy's leg, and once he had calmed down he still wanted to climb to the big cave. Pippi wove a rope from hibiscus stems and tied one end to a rock. Then she climbed as easily as a mountain goat over to the cave and fastened the other end there. And now even Annika dared to work her way across to the cave. When you had a secure rope to hold on to, it was no trouble at all.

The cave was wonderful. It was so big all the children could easily fit inside.

'This cave is almost better than our hollow oak back at Villa Villekulla,' said Tommy.

'No, not better, but just as good,' said Annika,

who felt a pang at the thought of that oak tree back home and didn't want to admit that there was anything better.

Momo showed the white children how many coconuts and breadfruit were stashed in the cave. You could live there for several weeks and not starve to death. Moana came up and showed them a hollowed-out bamboo cane that was crammed full of the most beautiful pearls. She gave Pippi, Tommy, and Annika a handful each.

'Pretty things you use for playing marbles in this country,' said Pippi.

It was lovely to sit in the cave and look out over the glittering sea. And it was very nice to lie on your stomach and spit down into the water. Tommy announced a long-spitting competition. Momo was a champion spitter, but even he couldn't beat Pippi. She had a way of propelling the spit between her front teeth that no one could match.

'If it starts drizzling in New Zealand today, it's my fault,' she said.

Tommy and Annika didn't do very well.

'White children no good spitting,' said Momo boastfully. He didn't really include Pippi among the white children.

'White children can't spit?' said Pippi. 'You
don't know what you're talking about. They
learn it in school from the very first class! Long-
spitting and high-spitting and jog-spitting. You
should see Tommy and Annika's teacher. Oh
my, how she can spit! She's got first prize for
jog-spitting. When she jogs around the town,
spitting, everyone cheers!'

'Uhh,' groaned Tommy and Annika.

Pippi raised a hand to her forehead and peered out over the water.

'There's a boat coming,' she said. 'A tiny little steamboat. I wonder what it's doing here?'

She might well wonder. The steamboat was approaching Koratuttutt Island at full speed. As well as some black sailors on board the boat, there were also two white men. Jim and Buck were their names. They were rough types who looked like real bandits. And that's exactly what they were.

Once, when Captain Longstocking had been buying tobacco in the shop on that other island, Jim and Buck had also been there. They had seen Captain Longstocking put a couple of unusually large and beautiful pearls on the counter, and they had overheard him say that on Koratuttutt Island the children played marbles with pearls like those. Ever since that day they'd had one single goal, and that was to travel to Koratuttutt Island and try to get their hands on those pearls. They knew Captain Longstocking was incredibly strong, and they also had great respect for the crew of the *Hoppetossa*, which is why they decided to seize their chance when all the men left to go hunting. Now their chance had come. Hidden behind a nearby island, they had watched through their telescopes as Captain Longstocking, his crew and all the Koratutt people paddled away from Koratuttutt Island. They waited until the canoes were well out of sight.

'Drop anchor!' shouted Buck, when the boat had almost reached the island. Pippi and the children watched them silently from up in the cave. The anchor was lowered overboard. Jim and Buck jumped into a dinghy and rowed to land. The black sailors were given orders to stay on board.

'Now we'll sneak up to the village and take them by surprise,' said Jim. 'Most likely it's only women and children at home.'

'Yes,' said Buck. 'But there were so many women in those canoes I would think only the children have been left behind. I hope they're playing marbles, hahaha.'

'Why?' shouted Pippi from the cave. 'Are you especially keen on playing marbles? Speaking personally, I prefer leapfrog.'

Jim and Buck wheeled round in astonishment

and saw Pippi and all the children poking their heads out of the cave. A delighted grin spread over their faces.

'Here we have the kids,' said Jim.

'Excellent,' said Buck. 'They won't give us no trouble, that's for sure.'

But even so, they decided to use some cunning. After all, they didn't know where the kids kept the pearls, so it was best to lure them by being friendly. They pretended that they hadn't come to Koratuttutt Island to take the pearls but only for a pleasant outing. They felt hot and sweaty, and Buck suggested they should start by having a swim.

'I'll just row back to the boat to get our swimming shorts,' he said.

And that's what he did. All the while Jim stood alone on the beach.

'Is this a good place to swim?' he called to the children in a smarmy voice.

'Absolutely splendid,' said Pippi. 'Absolutely splendid for sharks. They swim here every day.'

'Nonsense,' said Jim. 'I can't see any sharks.'

But it did worry him a little, and when Buck came back with the swimming shorts he told him what Pippi had said.

'A likely story,' said Buck. And he shouted to Pippi:

'Was it you who said it's dangerous to swim here?'

'Nope,' said Pippi. 'I never said that.'

'That's odd,' said Jim. 'Didn't you just say there might be sharks here?'

'Yes, that's what I said. But dangerous? I wouldn't go that far. My own grandad went swimming here last year.'

'Well, in that case,' said Buck.

'And Grandad got home from hospital last Friday,' Pippi continued. 'With the shapeliest pair of wooden legs ever to be seen on an old chap.'

She spat into the sea, looking thoughtful.

'So I wouldn't exactly say it was dangerous. But of course, a few arms and legs always get lost when people swim here. But as long as wooden legs cost less than one krona a pair, I don't think simple stinginess should stop you taking a nice healthy swim.'

She spat again.

'And my grandad is tickled pink with his

wooden legs. He says they're invaluable when he's going out to fight.'

'Do you know what I think?' said Buck. 'I think you're lying. Your grandad must be an old man. He wouldn't be going out fighting at his age.'

'Oh, wouldn't he!' Pippi squealed. 'He's the angriest old fellow to ever whack his opponent over the head with a wooden leg. He's never happy unless he's fighting from morning to evening. And if he can't fight he bites his nose in pure frustration.'

'What rubbish you talk,' said Buck. 'He can't bite himself on the nose.'

'Oh yes he can,' said Pippi. 'He stands on a chair.'

Buck thought about this for a moment, and then he swore and said:

'I'm not wasting any more time listening to your twaddle. Come on, Jim, let's get changed.'

'Just one more thing,' said Pippi. 'Grandad's got the longest nose in the world. He's got five parrots and they can all sit side by side on his nose!'

This made Buck absolutely furious.

'Do you know what, you little red-haired disaster, you are the most untruthful little kid I've ever met. You should be ashamed. Are you really trying to make me believe that five parrots can sit in a row on your grandad's nose? That's a lie, admit it!'

'Yes,' said Pippi, sorrowfully. 'It is a lie.'

'There you are!' said Buck. 'What did I tell you!'

'It's an awful, terrible lie,' said Pippi, even more sorrowfully.

'Yes, I knew it right away,' said Buck.

'Because the fifth parrot,' yelled Pippi, and burst into tears. 'The fifth parrot *has to stand on one leg.*'

'Go and jump in a lake,' said Buck, and he and Jim went behind a bush to get changed.

'Pippi, you haven't got a grandad,' said Annika, disapprovingly.

'Nope,' said Pippi. 'Do you have to?'

Buck was first to put on his swimming shorts. He dived elegantly from a rock into the sea and swam out. The children in the cave watched nervously. Then they spotted a shark's fin flash for a second above the surface of the water.

'Shark, shark!' shrieked Momo.

Buck, who was treading water and enjoying himself, turned his head and saw the dreadful predator coming towards him.

Probably no one has ever swum as fast as Buck did then. In a split second he reached land and shot out of the water. He was angry and scared, and he seemed to think it was Pippi's fault that there were sharks in the water.

'Are you mad, child!' he shouted. 'The sea's thick with sharks!'

'Did I say it wasn't?' said Pippi, putting her head sweetly on one side. 'I don't lie all the time, you understand.'

Jim and Buck went behind a bush and changed back into their clothes. They realized it was high time to start thinking about the pearls. Nobody knew how long Captain Longstocking and the others would stay away.

'Listen, kiddies,' said Buck. 'I heard someone say there was good pearl-fishing in these parts. Do you know if that's true?'

'I should say so,' said Pippi. 'The oysters positively crunch under your feet when you walk on the sea floor. Go down and see for yourselves.'

But Buck didn't want to do that.

'There are enormous pearls inside every single oyster,' said Pippi. 'Approximately like this.'

She held up a massive, shimmering pearl.

Jim and Buck were so excited they could hardly stand still.

'Have you got any more like that?' asked Jim. 'We'd really like to buy them from you.'

This wasn't true. Jim and Buck didn't have any money to buy pearls. They wanted to get them by tricking the children.

'Yep, we've got about five or six litres of pearls in this cave, at a guess,' said Pippi.

Jim and Buck could not disguise their delight.

'Marvellous,' said Buck. 'Bring them over here and we'll buy the lot.'

'Oh no,' said Pippi. 'Then what will the poor children use to play marbles with, do you suppose?'

A lot of discussion went on before Jim and Buck realized that they weren't going to get their hands on the pearls by trickery. But what they couldn't get by trickery, they would get by violence. Now at least they knew where the pearls were. All they had to do was climb across to the cave and fetch them.

Climb across to the cave—yes, that was the problem! During their bargaining Pippi had untied the hibiscus rope, just in case. It was now safe and sound in the cave.

Jim and Buck thought the way to the cave didn't look especially inviting, but clearly there was nothing for it.

'You do it, Jim,' said Buck.

'No, why don't you do it, Buck?' said Jim.

'*You do it, Jim,*' said Buck. He was stronger than Jim. So Jim started to climb. Desperately he clung to every little outcrop he could grab hold of. Cold sweat trickled down his back.

'Hold on tight, so you don't fall in,' said Pippi encouragingly.

Then Jim fell in. Buck shouted and swore from the beach. Jim shouted too, because he saw two sharks heading straight towards him. When they were no more than a metre away from him Pippi threw a coconut right under their noses. It scared them just long enough for Jim to swim to the water's edge and scramble up to the rocky shelf. His clothes were streaming with water and he looked a miserable sight. Buck told him off.

'Do it yourself, then you'll see how easy it is,' said Jim.

'Right, I'll show you how it's done,' said Buck, and he started to climb.

All the children watched him. Annika felt almost afraid as he got closer and closer.

'Oh-oh, don't step there or you'll fall in,' said Pippi.

'Where?' said Buck.

'There,' said Pippi, pointing. Buck looked down at his feet.

'We're getting through a lot of coconuts this way,' said Pippi a moment later, as she threw in another coconut to stop the sharks eating Buck, who was piteously thrashing about in the water. But out he came, livid with anger, and he wasn't afraid. He started climbing again straight away, because he was determined to reach the cave and get hold of the pearls.

This time it went better. When he was almost at the cave entrance he yelled out triumphantly:

'Now I'm going to give you what for!'

Then Pippi stuck out her finger and prodded him in the stomach.

"Splash," they heard.

'You might have taken the coconut with you when you went,' Pippi called after him as she hit a bullseye on the nose of a nearby shark. But more sharks turned up and she had to throw more coconuts. One of them happened to hit Buck on the head.

'Oh *crikey*, was that you?' said Pippi, when Buck gave a yell. 'From up here you look just like a nasty big shark.'

Jim and Buck decided to wait until the children gave in.

'They'll soon come toddling out when they get hungry enough,' Buck said grimly. 'Then I'll show them!'

He shouted to the children:

'I feel sorry for you, having to sit in that cave until you starve to death.'

'How kind-hearted you are,' said Pippi. 'But you don't have to worry for the first fourteen days. After that we might have to ration the coconuts.'

She cracked open a large coconut, drank the juice and ate the delicious flesh.

Jim and Buck swore. The sun was going down and they ought to be preparing to spend the night on the beach. They didn't dare row back to the steamer to sleep because then the children would get away and take the pearls with them. They lay down on the hard shelf of rock in their wet clothes. It was somewhat uncomfortable.

Up in the cave the children sat with sparkling eyes, eating coconuts and mashed breadfruit. The food was very tasty and everything was so nice and exciting. From time to time they poked out their heads to look at Jim and Buck. By now it was so dark they could only just make them out on the flat rock. But they could hear them swearing down there.

Suddenly there was a downpour of the very heaviest kind that only occurs in the tropics. Sheets of rain cascaded down from the sky. Pippi stuck the very furthest tip of her nose out of the cave.

'Could anyone be as lucky as you two?' she shouted to Jim and Buck.

'What do you mean by that?' asked Buck, hopefully. He thought perhaps the children had changed their minds and now wanted to give them the pearls. 'What do you mean, lucky?'

'Well, such extraordinary luck that you were

already wet through before this deluge arrived. Otherwise you would have been soaked in all this rain, wouldn't you?'

Someone was heard to swear down on the rocks, but it was impossible to tell whether it was Jim or Buck.

'Nighty-night, sleep well,' said Pippi. 'Because that's what we're going to do.'

The children all lay down on the floor of the cave. Tommy and Annika lay closest to Pippi and held her hand. They were very comfortable. It was perfectly warm and cosy in the cave. Outside, the rain poured down.

PIPPI GETS FED UP WITH JIM AND BUCK

The children slept well that night. Jim and Buck didn't. All they did was swear about the rain, and when it stopped raining they began arguing about whose fault it was that they hadn't been able to take the pearls, and who had actually come up with the stupid idea of going to Koratuttutt Island. But when the sun came up and dried their wet clothes and Pippi's cheery face appeared in the cave entrance wishing them good morning, they were more determined than ever to try and snatch the pearls and come away as rich men. The only problem was, they couldn't work out how to go about it.

All this time Pippi's horse had been wondering where Pippi and Tommy and Annika had got to. Mr Nilsson had returned from visiting his relatives in the jungle and he was wondering the same. He was also wondering what Pippi would say when she found out he had lost his little straw hat.

Mr Nilsson jumped up and sat on the horse's tail and off the horse trotted to look for Pippi. Eventually he came to the south side of the island and there he saw Pippi's head poking out of a cave. He neighed happily.

'Look, Pippi, here comes your horse!' shouted Tommy.

'With Mr Nilsson sitting on his tail!' shouted Annika.

Jim and Buck heard this. They heard that the horse coming along the beach belonged to Pippi, that red-haired disaster up in the cave.

Buck walked over and grabbed the horse by its mane.

'Listen to me, you troll spawn,' he yelled to Pippi. 'I'm going to kill your horse.'

'What, are you going to kill the horse I love so much?' said Pippi. 'My dear, sweet little horse. You don't mean it.'

'Yes I do. I'm afraid I'm going to have to,' said Buck. 'That is, unless you want to come down and hand over all the pearls. And I mean all of them! Otherwise your horse dies on the spot.'

Pippi looked at him seriously.

'Please,' she said. 'I'm asking you as nicely as I possibly can—don't kill my horse, and let the children keep their pearls.'

'You heard what I said,' Buck answered. 'Give us the pearls now, or else . . . !'

And he said in a low voice to Jim:

'Just wait till she gets here with the pearls. I'll beat her yellow and green to pay her back for this soaking wet night. As for the horse, we'll take it on board with us and sell it on some other island.'

He yelled to Pippi:

'Well, what's it to be? Are you coming down or not?'

'I suppose I'd better come down, in that case,' said Pippi. 'But don't forget, you asked me yourself.'

She skipped over the small rocky outcrops as easily as if they were the smoothest footpath, and then she jumped down to the flat rock where Jim and Buck and the horse were waiting. She stopped in front of Buck. There she stood, short and skinny, with the little piece of cloth wrapped around her waist and the two red plaits sticking out. Her eyes glowed menacingly.

'Where are the pearls, brat?' shouted Buck.

'There won't be any pearls today,' said Pippi. 'You'll be doing some leapfrogging instead.'

Then Buck let out a roar that made Annika tremble in the cave up above.

'Mark my words, I'll murder both you and your horse,' he shouted, and hurled himself at Pippi.

'Steady on, my good man,' said Pippi. She grabbed him round the waist and threw him three metres up in the air. He hit the rock with quite a wallop when he landed. Suddenly Jim came to life. He aimed a vicious blow at Pippi but she stepped aside with a delighted chuckle. The next second it was Jim's turn to fly up into the bright morning sky. And there they both were, Jim and Buck, sitting on the rock and groaning loudly. Pippi walked over and picked them up, one in each fist.

'It isn't *healthy* to be so obsessed with playing marbles as you seem to be,' she said. 'There has to be *some* limit to your need for enjoyment.'

She carried them to the dinghy and threw them in.

'Now go home and ask your mum for five öre for marbles,' she said. 'I guarantee they're just as good.'

Shortly afterwards the steamboat chugged away from Koratuttutt Island. It has never been seen in those waters since.

Pippi stroked her horse. Mr Nilsson jumped up onto her shoulder. And around the furthest tip of the island appeared a long row of canoes.

It was Captain Longstocking and his company, returning home after a successful hunting trip. Pippi called out and waved at them and they waved back with their oars.

Then Pippi quickly tied the rope in place so Tommy and Annika and the others could leave the cave. And when the canoes came alongside the *Hoppetossa* in the little bay soon afterwards, the flock of children stood waiting to welcome them.

Captain Longstocking patted Pippi.

'All been peaceful while we were away?' he asked.

'Totally peaceful,' said Pippi.

'No it wasn't, Pippi,' said Annika. 'There were nearly accidents.'

'Oh yes, I forgot about that,' said Pippi. 'It wasn't exactly peaceful, Daddy Ephraim. As soon as you turn your back all sorts of things happen.'

'Oh, my dear child, what happened?' asked Captain Longstocking, anxiously.

'Something terrible,' said Pippi. 'Mr Nilsson lost his straw hat.'

PIPPI LEAVES KORATUTTUTT ISLAND

Blissful days followed, blissful days in a warm blissful world full of sun and glittering blue water and fragrant flowers.

Tommy and Annika were so brown by now that you could scarcely see any difference between them and the Koratutt children. And Pippi had freckles on precisely every single speck of her face.

'This trip is an absolute beauty treatment for me,' she said, contentedly. 'I am frecklier and more beautiful than ever. If it carries on like this I'll be downright irresistible.'

In actual fact, Momo and Moana and all the other Koratutt children already thought Pippi was irresistible. They had never had so much fun before, and they liked Pippi as much as Tommy and Annika did. Oh, they liked Tommy and Annika too, of course, and Tommy and Annika liked them in return. That's why they had such a nice time together, every one of them, and they played and played all and every day. They often spent time in the cave. Pippi had taken blankets there so they could stay the night whenever they wanted, and it was even more comfortable than the first night. She had also made a rope ladder that reached right down to the water, and all the children climbed up and down the rope ladder and swam and splashed about to their heart's content. And yes, they could swim there now. Pippi had made a barrier out of fishing net so the sharks couldn't get at them. It was such fun swimming in and out of caves that were full of water. And even Tommy and Annika had learned to dive for oysters. The first pearl Annika found was a large and beautiful pink one. She decided to take it home with her and make it into a ring which she would keep to remind her of Koratuttutt Island.

Sometimes they pretended that Pippi was Buck, trying to get into the cave to steal the pearls. Tommy would pull up the rope ladder leaving

Pippi to scramble up the cliff as best she could. All the children would shout: 'Buck's coming, Buck's coming,' when she poked her head in the cave, and one by one they were allowed to prod her in the stomach and send her plunging backwards into the sea. Then she would splash about with only her feet above the surface of the water, and the children laughed so much they very nearly tumbled out of the cave.

When they grew tired of playing there, they could be in their bamboo hut. Pippi and the children had built it together, although Pippi had done most of it, of course. It was large and perfectly square and made of bamboo poles, and they could climb about inside it and over it exactly as they pleased. Right next to the hut grew a tall coconut tree. Pippi had chopped steps into the trunk so that they could climb all the way to the top. There was a very fine view from up there. Between two other palm trees Pippi had hung a swing made of hibiscus stems. It was absolutely perfect. If you swung really high and at the very highest point hurled yourself off, you would land in the water. Pippi swung terrifyingly high and she flew so far out into the water that she said:

'One of these days I'll plop down in Australia, and someone's going to get an unpleasant surprise when I land on their head.'

The children also made expeditions into the jungle. There was a high mountain there and a waterfall that hurtled down a steep mountainside. Pippi had decided to ride down the waterfall in a barrel, and she did it, too. She brought along one of the barrels from the *Hoppetossa*, and crept inside. Momo and Tommy closed the lid and helped to push the barrel over the waterfall. It bounced down at spectacular speed and eventually it broke. The children all saw Pippi disappear in the masses of water and they thought they would never see her again. But all of a sudden she popped up, stepped onto dry land and said:

'They go pretty fast, these barrels.'

And so the days passed, one after the other. But soon the rainy season would arrive, and when that happened Captain Longstocking used to shut himself in his cabin and contemplate life, and because of that he was afraid Pippi wouldn't like being on Koratuttutt Island any more. Tommy and Annika found themselves thinking more often about their mum and dad at home. They also wanted to be home in time for Christmas. That was why they weren't as sad as you might imagine when Pippi said one morning:

'Tommy and Annika, how about going home to Villa Villekulla for a while?'

Of course, for Momo and Moana and the other Koratutt children it was a sad day when they watched Pippi and Tommy and Annika board the *Hoppetossa* to sail home. But Pippi promised they would return lots of times to Koratuttutt Island. The Koratutt children had woven goodbye garlands of white flowers to hang around the necks of Pippi and Tommy and Annika, and their farewell song floated mournfully over the water as the boat sailed away. Captain Longstocking was standing on the beach with them. He had to stay and rule over his people. Instead, Fridolf had taken on the job of sailing the children home. Captain Longstocking solemnly blew his nose in his large handkerchief and waved goodbye. Pippi and Tommy and Annika cried so much the tears positively squirted from their eyes, and they waved and waved to Captain Longstocking and the small Koratutt children until they were out of sight.

They had a steady following wind all the way home.

'We'd better get out your winter jumpers in plenty of time before we reach the North Sea,' said Pippi.

'Ugh, yes,' said Tommy and Annika.

It was soon clear that despite the steady wind they couldn't possibly be home in time for Christmas. Tommy and Annika were very sad to hear that. Imagine, no Christmas tree and no Christmas presents!

'We might as well have stayed on Koratuttutt Island,' said Tommy, sulkily.

Annika thought of her mother and father and felt she wanted to go home anyway. But it was a pity they would miss Christmas, both Tommy and Annika agreed on that.

One dark evening at the beginning of January, Pippi, Tommy, and Annika could make out the lights of the little town shining out to them. They were home.

'Well, so much for *that* South Sea trip,' said Pippi, as she strode down the gangplank with the horse.

No one had come to meet them because no

one could possibly have known when they were coming home. Pippi lifted Tommy, Annika and Mr Nilsson onto the horse and off they rode to Villa Villekulla. The horse had to work hard as he plodded home because the streets and lanes were full of snow. Tommy and Annika stared ahead through the whirling snowflakes. Soon they would be at home with their mum and dad, and all of a sudden they realized they were longing to see them.

The Settergren house was lit up so invitingly, and through the window Tommy and Annika could see their parents sitting at the dinner table.

'There's Mum and Dad,' said Tommy, and he sounded very pleased as he said it.

But Villa Villekulla was in darkness and the snow was piled up around it.

Annika was upset at the thought of Pippi going in there alone.

'Please, Pippi, come and stay with us the first night,' she said.

'Oh, no,' said Pippi, and dropped down into the snow outside the gate. 'I've got some sorting out to do in Villa Villekulla.'

She waded through the deep snow drifts that

came all the way up to her waist. The horse trudged after her.

'But think how cold it will be indoors,' said Tommy. 'There hasn't been any heating on for ages.'

'Huh,' said Pippi. 'As long as your heart is warm and ticks like it should, you won't freeze.'

PIPPI LONGSTOCKING DOESN'T WANT TO GROW UP

Oh, how Tommy and Annika's mum and dad hugged their children and clapped them on the back and kissed them and laid the table with a delicious dinner for them and then tucked them up in their beds at bedtime! And they sat for a long, long time on the edge of their beds and listened to the children's stories of all the extraordinary things that had happened on Koratuttutt Island. They were all very happy. There was only one thing that bothered them, and that was Christmas. Tommy and Annika didn't want to tell their mum and dad that they were sad about coming home too late for the Christmas tree and the Christmas presents, but they were. It felt strange coming back, the way it always does when you have been away, and it would have helped enormously if only there had been Christmas to look forward to when they got home.

It also made Tommy and Annika upset to think about Pippi. By now she was inside Villa Villekulla with her feet on the pillow and no one there to tuck her in. They decided to go round and see her as soon as they could the following day.

But the next day their mother didn't want to let them go because she hadn't seen them for such a long time, and anyway their granny was coming for dinner, to welcome the children home. Tommy and Annika wondered anxiously what Pippi would be doing all day, and when it started to get dark that evening they couldn't stand it any longer.

'Please, Mum, we've simply *got* to go and see Pippi,' said Tommy.

'Well, off you go then,' said Mrs Settergren. 'But don't stay too long.'

So Tommy and Annika ran off.

When they came to Villa Villekulla's garden gate they stopped and stared. It looked exactly like a Christmas card. The whole house was nestled so softly in the snow and every window shone brightly. On the veranda a torch was flaming and it cast its light far over the carpet of snow outside. A path had been carefully cleared up to the veranda, so Tommy and Annika didn't have to wade through any snowdrifts.

Just as they were stamping the snow off their shoes on the veranda, the door opened and there stood Pippi.

'Happy Christmas, one and all,' she said. Then she led them into the kitchen. And there, would you believe it, stood a Christmas tree! The candles were lit and seventeen sparklers crackled and glowed and spread their familiar smell around them. The table had been laid with rice pudding and ham and sausages and all sorts of Christmas treats, even gingerbread men and sugary doughnuts. A fire flickered in the hearth and the horse was standing beside the log box, politely scraping his hoof on the floor. Mr Nilsson scuttled to and fro in the tree between the sparklers.

'He's supposed to be a Christmas angel,' said Pippi sternly, 'but can I get him to sit still? Oh no!'

Tommy and Annika stood there, speechless.

'Ooh, Pippi,' breathed Annika. 'It's so wonderful! How did you have time to do all this?'

'I have an industrious nature,' said Pippi.

All of a sudden Tommy and Annika felt overwhelmingly happy.

'I think it's good to be back in Villa Villekulla again,' said Tommy.

They sat round the table and ate heaps of ham and rice pudding and sausages and gingerbread men, and they thought it all tasted much better than bananas and breadfruit.

'But you know, Pippi, Christmas has gone now,' said Tommy.

'Oh no it hasn't,' said Pippi. 'Villa Villekulla's calendar is running a little late. I must take it to the calendar-maker's and get it adjusted. That'll put some life into it.'

'How lovely,' said Annika. 'We're having Christmas after all. But without Christmas presents, of course.'

'Oh, I'm glad you mentioned that,' said Pippi. 'I've hidden your Christmas presents. You'll have to look for them yourselves.'

Tommy and Annika's faces went pink with delight and they shot up from the table and started looking. In the log box Tommy found a parcel with 'TOMMY' written on it. It was a brilliant box of paints. And under the table Annika found a parcel with her name on it, and inside the parcel was a beautiful red parasol.

'I can take this with me next time we go to Koratuttutt Island,' said Annika. Two parcels were tucked under the mantelpiece. In one was a little jeep for Tommy and in the other a doll's tea service for Annika. And hanging from the horse's tail was a tiny, tiny parcel, and inside was a clock that Tommy and Annika could have in their room.

When they had found all the presents they thanked Pippi with an enormous hug. She stood by the kitchen window, looking at all the snow in the garden.

'Tomorrow we'll build a big snow house,' she said. 'And in the evening we'll light candles inside.'

'Oh, yes, let's do that!' said Annika, feeling more and more delighted to be home.

'I've been wondering if it's possible to make a ski run from the roof down to the snowdrifts,' said Pippi. 'I'm planning to teach the horse to ski, but I can't work out if he needs four skis or two.'

'We'll have so much fun tomorrow,' said

Tommy. 'What luck we came home in the middle of the Christmas holiday.'

'We'll always have fun,' said Annika. 'Here in Villa Villekulla and on Koratuttutt Island and everywhere.'

Pippi nodded in agreement. They had climbed up onto the kitchen table, all three. Suddenly a dark shadow fell over Tommy's face.

'I never want to grow up,' he said firmly.

'Not me, either,' said Annika.

'No, it's nothing to long for,' said Pippi. 'Grown-ups never have any fun. All they've got is masses of boring old work and stupid clothes and corns and dinkum tax.'

'Income tax, you mean,' said Annika.

'Same old bunkum, anyway,' said Pippi. 'And they're full of superstition and shenanigans. They believe there'll be a horrendous accident if they happen to put a knife in their mouth when they're eating, and stuff like that.'

'And they've no idea how to play,' said Annika. 'Ugh, to think you've got to grow up!'

'Who says you have to?' asked Pippi. 'If I remember rightly, I've got a few pills somewhere.'

'What sort of pills?' asked Tommy.

'Some very good pills for people who don't want to be grown-ups,' said Pippi, and she jumped down from the table. She searched in every drawer and box, and after a short while she was back with something that looked remarkably like three dried yellow peas.

'Peas?' said Tommy, in astonishment.

'That's what you think,' said Pippi. 'These are no peas. These are squiggle pills. An old Indian chief in Rio gave them to me ages ago when I happened to mention I wasn't that keen on growing up.'

'And those little pills help?' Annika asked doubtfully.

'Oh yes,' Pippi assured her. 'But they have to be eaten in the dark and you have to say this:

Oh my dear little squiggle
Don't let me grow any biggle.'

'Surely you mean *bigger*,' said Tommy.

'If I said "biggle" then I mean "biggle",' said Pippi. 'That's the trick, you see. Most people say "bigger" and that's the worst thing you can do, because then you start growing faster than ever.

There was a boy once who swallowed these pills. He said "bigger" instead of "biggle" and he started growing fast enough to give you the heebie-jeebies. Several metres a day, he grew. It was an awful pity. I suppose it was quite convenient so long as he could eat apples straight off the branches like a giraffe. But that didn't work for long because he grew too tall. When little old ladies came to visit him at home and tried to say, "My, how big and clever you've grown", they had to shout it through a megaphone so he could hear. All you could see of him were his long spindly legs disappearing into the clouds like two flagpoles. No one heard of him again. Oh yes, there was one time, when he decided to lick the sun and got blisters on his tongue, and then he wailed so loudly all the flowers down on earth shrivelled up and died. But that was his last sign of life. Although his legs still wander around down there in Rio, playing havoc with the traffic, I shouldn't wonder.'

'I don't dare swallow any pills,' said Annika, sounding frightened. 'In case I say the wrong thing.'

'You won't say the wrong thing,' Pippi comforted her. 'If I thought you would do that,

I wouldn't give you any pills. It would be rather boring having only your legs to play with. Tommy, me and your legs—some company that would be.'

'Phooey, Annika, you won't say it wrong,' said Tommy.

They blew out the Christmas tree candles and the kitchen went completely dark, apart from the glow of the logs burning in the stove. They sat silently in a circle in the middle of the floor and held hands. Pippi gave Tommy and Annika one squiggle pill each. They felt a shiver of excitement run down their spines. Imagine, any second now that curious little pill would be in their stomachs, and then they would never, ever need to grow up. It was wonderful.

'Now,' Pippi whispered.

They swallowed their pills.

> 'Oh my dear little squiggle
> Don't let me grow any biggle,'

all three said together.

♥

It was done. Pippi switched on the light.

'Marvellous,' she said. 'Now we won't have to be

big and get corns and other troublesome things. Although the pills have been in my cupboard for so long I'm not *entirely* sure they still work. But we'll hope for the best.'

Something had occurred to Annika.

'Oh, Pippi,' she said. 'You were going to be a pirate when you grow up.'

'Hah, I can be a pirate anyway,' said Pippi. 'I can be a tiny weeny ferocious pirate, spreading death and confusion all around.'

She thought for a moment.

'Just think,' she said. 'What if a lady walks past in years to come and sees us playing in the garden. She might say to Tommy: "How old are you, young fellow?" And you might say: "Fifty-three, if I'm not mistaken."'

Tommy chuckled.

'Then she'll think I'm very small for my age,' he said.

'That's true,' Pippi admitted. 'But then you can say you were bigger when you were younger.'

At that moment Tommy and Annika remembered what their mum had said about not staying too long.

'We'd better go home now,' said Tommy.

'But we'll be back tomorrow,' said Annika.

'Good,' said Pippi. 'We'll start on the snow house at eight o'clock.'

She walked with them to the gate, and her red plaits bobbed about her head as she ran back to Villa Villekulla.

♥

'Do you know what?' said Tommy later, when he was brushing his teeth. 'Do you know, if I hadn't known they were squiggle pills, I'd bet anything they were normal peas.'

Annika was standing by the window in her pink pyjamas, gazing towards Villa Villekulla.

'Look, I can see Pippi!' she called out, in delight.

Tommy hurried over to the window. Yes, it was true! Now that the trees had lost their leaves they could see directly into Pippi's kitchen.

Pippi was sitting at her kitchen table with her head propped in her hands. With a far-away expression she was staring at a small candle flickering on the table in front of her.

'She . . . she looks so lonely, somehow,' said Annika, and her voice trembled. 'Oh Tommy, if only it was tomorrow and we could go over to her now, straight away.'

They stood there quietly, looking out at the winter night. The stars shone down over Villa Villekulla's roof. Inside was Pippi. She would always be there. That was a wonderful thought. The years would go by but Pippi, Tommy, and Annika wouldn't grow up. Unless the squiggle pills had lost their power, of course! New springs and summers would come, and new autumns and winters, but they would carry on playing. Tomorrow they would build a snow house and make a ski slope from Villa Villekulla's roof, when spring came they would climb inside the hollow oak where the lemonade bottles grew, they would play at being thing-finders and they would ride on Pippi's horse, they would sit in the log box and tell stories, they might even go to Koratuttutt Island sometimes to say hello to Momo and Moana and the others, but they would always return to Villa Villekulla. Yes, it was a truly comforting thought—Pippi would be in Villa Villekulla forever.

'If only she'd look this way, we could wave at her,' said Tommy.

But Pippi only stared straight ahead, dreaming.

Then she blew out the candle.

OTHER ADVENTURES

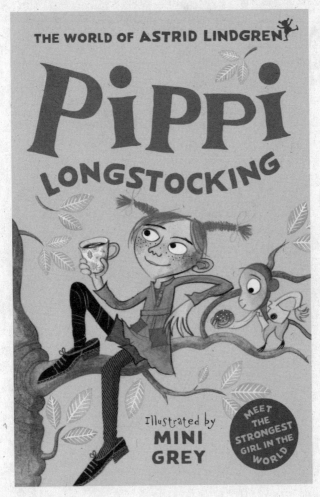

Everything's fun with Pippi around! Pippi Longstocking is one of the best loved characters of all time. She's funny, feisty, and has the most amazing adventures!

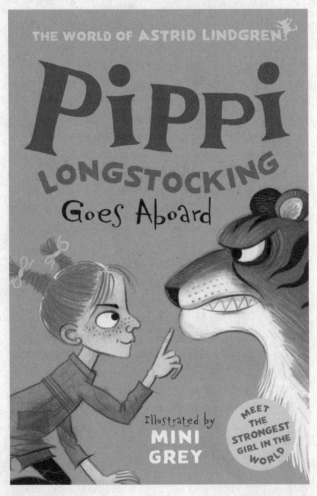

Pippi is back and as crazy and as funny as ever! But for Tommy and Annika, the fun might stop all too soon if Pippi agrees to go back to sea with her father.

ABOUT THE AUTHOR

Astrid Lindgren was born in 1907, and grew up at a farm called Näs in the south of Sweden. Her first book was published in 1944, followed a year later by *Pippi Longstocking*. She wrote 34 chapter books and 41 picture books, that all together have sold 165 million copies worldwide. Her books have been translated into 107 different languages and according to UNESCO's annual list, she is the 18th most translated author in the world.

She created stories about Pippi, a free-spirited, red-haired girl, to entertain her daughter, Karin, who was ill with pneumonia. The girl's name 'Pippi Longstocking' was in fact invented by Karin. Astrid Lindgren once commented about her work, 'I write to amuse the child within me, and can only hope that other children may have some fun that way, too.'

For more information visit www.astridlindgren.com